Cocteau's
Invitation

by
I0608008

Erik Martiny

River Boat Books

Cocteau's Invitation
Copyright © 2019, 2023 by Erik Martiny

Translated by the author from *Ne soyez pas timide*.
First published in Paris by Les Editions Pierre-Guillaume de Roux, 2019.

The painting adapted for the cover artwork is titled "Portrait of Ambroise Vollard" by Pablo Picasso (1910). The painting is now housed in the Pushkin Museum in Moscow.

Printed in the United States of America.
Published by River Boat Books, St. Paul, MN.
First printing Septmber 9, 2023.

ISBN: 978-1-955823-15-9

In memory of my father, a great lover of words.

Cocteau's Invitation

"*Living is a horizontal fall.*
                    —*Jean Cocteau, Opium*

*If your house was on fire and you could
only take one thing, what would you take?
Cocteau: the fire.*
                    —*Jean Cocteau, Interviews*

CONTENTS

The Neighbours

I

An egg. A shell. That's what you think when you see him on the other side of the fence. He stays there, motionless before you, outside of time. He contemplates you, smiling, his mouth set with ivory teeth, his eyes sparkling with jasper. A Fabergé egg.

He's staring at me right now, overcome with bliss, as if I were an undiscovered animal, an incomprehensible and fascinating thing.

I've never seen anyone capable of expressing such rapture. When I say "hello", he is overcome with felicity, as if I've just managed to compress the most beautiful poems in the French language into a single word.

He lingers, watching me, and I know that if I don't indicate I'm about to leave, he'll remain there, rooted to the spot indefinitely, his face caught in the overbite of his grin.

He hasn't responded to my greeting so I ask him if he'd like a few lemons from the garden.

Still without an answer, I take one out of my basket to illustrate the word.

I hold the citrus fruit in my hand for close to twenty seconds before he grasps the overall significance of the lemon.

Abruptly coming back to life again, he starts rubbing his head as if he has forgotten when he went almost entirely bald.

"Wait ... let me call my wife!"

I happen to know the person he's just mentioned. She's my next-door neighbour—a real chatterbox who makes the most of every opportunity to knead my brain with interminable, cyclical sentences.

"Please don't disturb her! I'll come and hand them to you. Don't move, stay where you are!"

"Oh, how nice of you!"

I clamber down in haste from the tree, painfully cutting my thigh on a chipped branch.

"You know what, I have more than enough citrus fruit. Here, you can make hot lemon drinks in the evening, if your wife doesn't make you some lemon cake."

"Why, thank you, sir! Oh...but goodness, there's blood running down your leg. Hang on, I'll go and get you some antiseptic for that! We have all sorts of bottles for fighting germs."

"Please, please don't bother. You're very kind, but really. It's—there's no need, honestly."

"You've had your tetanus shot? Same...here!"

He looks at my thigh, mesmerized by the red streak trickling down from under my shorts, as if realizing I'm also merely human after all.

His face darkens. Gazing vacantly, he looks up at the branches of the lemon tree, as if he has forgotten I'm there. His eyes glaze over, his irises melting into the whites. His pupils are greyer than usual. He stays there contemplating the cut in my leg as if he's deciphering a dark omen. He stares into the wound as if delving into the abyss.

I interrupt his day dream to hand him the lemons. He stares at them wistfully, his eyebrows lifted a little, bemused by the yellow enigma. I stare at the still life of the two lemons placed on the skin of his hands, pale and puffy as button mushrooms, and I suddenly feel overcome with sadness for a man rendered grotesque by the wear and tear of time. I have no idea what his life was like, but I imagine it was dull and uneventful, a prim and proper life, all tidy and clean like his little house full of identical shelves covered in uninteresting trinkets, surrounded by bare walls and grey, rectilinear tiles.

He was a regional inspector in his day, which is something of note, if you think about it, but I picture him being uncreative in the role. Full of bourgeois kindliness, stilted and complacent, straitlaced, with ties like nooses round his neck. I see him sitting at the back of the classroom, a sort of amiable gravedigger, an employee of the French State's educational funeral home, tasked with the writing of death certificates for the teaching body, as the received expression goes, and the placing of the professorial corpse in the coffin.

If *Le Petit Robert* is to be believed—I have the dictionary in my hands at this very moment—a clone is "the descendant of an individual by vegetative multiplication". Exactly what I had in mind. When you enter the monoclonal world of teaching—don't think you'll be spared, sooner or later, everyone ends up being absorbed by the French education system—you too will find yourself sucked in by its molecules. Your personal identity will be annihilated. You'll conform to the copy and find you have been turned into a photocopier. If you inadvertently, or willingly, feel yourself drifting towards teaching (this actually does happen on occasion), get a grip. There's still time. Even if you find yourself in front of the door that brings you face to face with a board of examiners.

But I see you, and I know that I am wasting my time, because you're going to enter that room anyway, your clammy hand trembling on the door handle, even though you know you're going to confront an assembly of undertakers. For the vibe is always tuned to such a high degree of jubilation among the members of the panel that you get the feeling you are entering a funerary chamber where people are on the point of committing some mysteriously ritualized primitive sacrifice. The silence is dense, opaque.

You enter the professorial womb and you know that your life is suspended by a cord.

Please forgive my recourse to wordplay and digressions. I can't help myself. You sometimes hear in semi-learned circles—occasionally high up in the hierarchy—that "literature and puns don't make good bedfellows". Some of my French literature colleagues actually believe this, some publishers do too. They'd like to prevent words from coupling, lay down deadly serious hard-and-fast rules in the only arena in which it should be forbidden to forbid (I admit with a certain pride that I was conceived on the 3rd of May 1968, the day the Sorbonne was taken by storm, in a corner of the Richelieu auditorium).

These censors behave as if Rabelais, Shakespeare, Joyce, Beckett, Nabokov, Kristeva, Cixous (not to mention all the rest) had never given in to the sin of wordplay, as if the modernist revolution hadn't freed literature from the asphyxiating stranglehold of all those old prescriptive rules. They'd like to lay down the law as if they were in politics, set up no-go zones, impose literary taboos. They'd like to authorize only the smoothest, plainest, risk-free, humdrum style, devoid of over-daring metaphor and any strong flavours. Lexical spices are no longer considered decent in the current climate.

In most French schools these days, you witness an overwhelming return to literary gentility and the manacles of decorum. When

I let my colleagues know that I sometimes put books like *Justine, or the Misfortunes of Virtue, Story of the Eye, Lolita,* or even Agota Kristof's *The Notebook* on my courses, they look at me as if I've lost my marbles.

To condemn this kind of literary freedom, people readily quote Victor Hugo when, using the character of Tholomyès in *The Wretched* as a spokesperson, he says that wordplay is "the bird dropping of the mind in flight". Those same people forget the fact that Hugo goes on to defend the usefulness and vitality of word games as a fundamental right: "The joke falls where it will; after excreting its silliness, the spirit ascends the azure sky. The whitish stain that spatters the rock does not keep the condor from soaring. Far be it from me to insult the pun! I honour it according to its merits, no more. The most noble, sublime and charming beings within the realm of humanity, and perhaps beyond it, have resorted to wordplay", and so on.

Writing is all about fiddling with words, mistreating them, rubbing them together. Above all else, toying with words is a kind of joyous, playful, whimsical micro-digression in my view, but square Cartesians don't like rambling either. My classes are full of embedded digressions. As you will see, I'm soon going to disappear to make way for a digression so long it buries the main plot.

*　　　*　　　*　　　*　　　*　　　*

I've come to the realization I'm being a bit hard on my poor neighbour. You may not have sensed it straight away, but I have a certain affection for him, despite everything I've said. If you put things in perspective, I may be entirely wrong about him. His life may have been full of excitement and teeming with secrets: a passing lover, wet dreams at night (in the daytime?), forbidden reading behind the locked restroom door with his spouse's attentive (erotic?) ear glued to the door, a trip to an exotic land with permissive dealings under the guise of an inspector's mission? Anything is possible, really. Is there not a glimmer of lost naughtiness huddled at the back of his senescent stare? Is not advanced old age, in the final analysis, but a thick shroud placed over a jack-in-the-box coffin?

Frankly, I don't know. Whatever the case, my neighbour's daily life is as neat and tidy as a musical score, the whole thing directed by his conductor of a wife. I have to tell you that Mrs. Hearse (that's their surname—oh the joyful hand of chance) relishes Order. Everything is not only tidied away in her home, things are cross checked, calculated, cleaned, dusted off, bleached, cleared of mosquitoes, sanitised, combed, measured with the utmost precision. There isn't an eyelash out of place. I sometimes

wonder if they don't avoid sleeping in the
master bed so they don't crease the sheets.
Eating seems out of the question: in fact, you
only have to see Mr. Hearse's hollow face to be
sure of that.

I see I've become a little cynical. It helps to
pass the time. If they knew how merciless I am,
they'd certainly be mortified. I'm not really sure
what pushes me to adopt such a niggardly view.
Recent events are no doubt the reason. I find
refuge in Schadenfreude so I don't get sucked
down in the doldrums. It's a well-known fact,
cynics are fallen romantics.

I have to tell you I carry within me a form
of what the books call chronic mourning. An
existential wound that ravages my soul and
grips me by the guts like a murderous form of
jealousy. I feel utterly cored. An eagle flies off
me every morning, my gutted liver in its talons.
Putting it that way is barely an exaggeration.

A few months ago, I would never have
thought that a feeling of that nature could lay
hold of me, not at my age. An old fogey like me.
And yet, when I wake up at night, absolute loss
tears through my veins like venom. I struggle
in the dark. I sometimes have to hold on to the
bedposts for dear life, so I don't throw myself
out the window, so I don't fly apart. Imprisoned
by the bed 'til daybreak, I get up, undone,
utterly exhausted, a broken shell. I find myself
obliged to stick myself together, piece by piece:

pants, shirt, sock, the other sock, shoe, the other shoe, the face.

More or less glued together, I go out to the bakery. I proffer a fake smile to the cashier in exchange for a loaf. I go home. Butter my bread. I let the tea brew. I drink it like a good lad. I follow Mrs. Hearse's good example. I try to put some order in my life so it doesn't fall apart, so the wall stays standing until I find something that will shore it up.

The story of my loss is hard to recount.

I can tell practically nobody. Everyone I know has cast the stone of disapproval. Even my friends refuse to understand me. If I told Mrs. Hearse about it at one sitting, she would probably have a canary.

The way I am now, I'm beginning to understand what those filmmakers accused of misconduct must feel. Outside the prison-world, they are nevertheless condemned to see their lives reduced to a few seconds, a few minutes of reprehensible behaviour. Their whole lives, their work, their entire being reduced to nothing over a few unfortunate minutes. They're perceived as monsters by the public, nothing more. Admired so greatly in the past, even their films as viewed as monstrous. People refuse to see them.

Sentenced to life, these condemned men would no doubt like those few moments of wayward behaviour to be edited out. It's the exact opposite that happens. Their whole life

becomes a silent movie condemned to play in
a continuous loop a snippet of private life that
should never have happened.

In the eyes of those I know, I'm more or
less viewed like those ill-fated film directors.
Especially in the eyes of my pupils' parents.
The only major difference is that I don't regret
a thing. On the contrary. My fatal decision, my
misguided moment is the best thing that ever
happened to me.

Seen from the outside, admittedly, I'll
acknowledge that my story is questionable
to say the least. Here are the bare facts: fifty-
year-old (past his prime) teacher sleeps with
fifteen-year-old (virgin) pupil.

I agree.

I admit I deserve to be looked at askance.
Put that bluntly, I too perceive myself through
a different lens. I become an unscrupulous,
cynical type. Gone is the will to identify with
me; gone the reader's sympathy.

But let's mull over that. Even a fictional
character with half of my flaws (a hint of
self-importance for instance) will cause readers
to withdraw allegiance and compassion. A
character who is a little vile, slightly gross, a bit
of a grease bag might make it, but a narrator
who canvases as happy to be immoral is much
harder to swallow. Which is why I'm going
to make myself a little less odious, without
massaging the facts too much, without giving

up too much in the name of propriety or the conventional beauty of stories in which the main characters are all decent and dignified. I want the characters in this tale to remain sufficiently unlovable and grotesque because I feel that the refusal of the ridiculous (which is particularly developed in homo sapiens) is one of the greatest shortcomings of our species and without a doubt the greatest limitation in the quest for beauty and the realisation of our potential. It's the quirky experiences that allow us to entirely fly by the nets of conformity, received wisdom and cerebral cloning.

More than a philosophy, however, I'd like to offer an aesthetic of the grotesque, to depict the beauty hidden behind situations that seem laughable on the surface. In a word, if you favour conventional relationships, if you only favour likeable, admirable characters, stop reading. Close this book on the spot, put it back discreetly on the pile in front of you, because I won't promise to stop at the title of the next section.

The Milk of Human Kindness

II

Ludmilla was sixteen.

An extra year helps—the image of the pupil seems more feminine, hairs start to sprout.

Ludmilla was in her final school year and therefore precocious, not to say over-gifted. Her greater maturity compared to her classmates was in fact palpable on every level. She was more thoughtful, deeper than her peers, more physically developed too: her breasts were full of sap, her flavescent vagina lodged like honey in the hollow of a tree.

While her body and spirit were, so to speak, as developed as those of a woman, what I savoured the most (and I admit this without blushing in the least), were the residues of childhood that still floated about her. Her delicate, little-girl fragrance awakened memories and sensations that I thought had disappeared forever: her breath sweet as a lollypop, her feet smelling like the ear of a new-born baby. Forgotten also was that silky, satin skin that you don't even notice as an amorous teen, getting gradually used to the rough caresses of middle age without even realizing.

My psychologist maintains that paedophilia is a form of nostalgia. In his view, all men become paedophiles as they get older, especially those who don't act on their desires because their bottled up drives start to increase. The proof of this theory he says is the number of parents who kiss their children directly on the mouth, the number of men who ask (or do not dare to ask) their partner to wax their swimsuit area and the pussy beside it, the number of women who do it spontaneously under the pretext that hairs might cross the bikini line (he calls that auto-paedophilia in women).

He says it's normal to want to penetrate and possess absolute beauty, beauty in its purest form. You just have to avoid attempting to possess it under duress, so as not to break beauty and end up in the ugliness of a prison.

You are thus not born a paedophile, you become one. It's in the natural order of things. Simone de Beauvoir acknowledged that as a teacher: every year, she would choose a junior school pupil with praiseworthy results and teach her the art of sex, placing her thereafter in the care of Jean-Paul Sartre. For outstanding end of term results the reward was philo-sophical cunnilingus and closed proceedings with Jean-Paul and his pecker. Just imagine the degree of motivation amongst pupils to excel in the subject of philosophy! Their progress at the end of the year must have been quite phenomenal.

And thus with some abnegation she provided her paedophilic pedagogy, a sort of generous, self-sacrificing paedophilia, in keeping with those Asian grandmothers who suck the penises of infants to appease their colic and teething pains, their troubled sleep.

The issue of beauty set aside, there is probably an element of more or less conscious transgressive joy felt by most people who harbour this fantasy, this over-pronounced contrastive aesthetic: the hairy, crusty beast yoking itself to the lovely, untouched, hairless skin; seasoned experience feeding itself by rubbing off disarmed innocence, the soon-to-be-dead person latching feverishly onto the early stages of life.

The thing that personally motivates me the most, by a long shot, is rediscovering the child I used to be, it's diving back to a time when life was fresh and full of sap, stuffed with illusion, a time when life was gorged with aspirational meaning.

But I agree with my shrink: genuine paedophiles love children enough to leave them unharmed. Which is why I would probably not have signed the plea written up by the French

intellectuals who tried to legalize inter-gen-
erational relationships in the 1970s. I don't
like power imbalances and your average child
molester is usually more muscular and given to
entrapping than his partners are.

The only possible paedophilia in my view
therefore involves whole-hearted consent. It was
Ludmilla who came up to me; she was also the
first to interfere. I simply gave into her overture.
And in any case she had already reached the
age of consent when she presented herself to
me. When all's said and done, it's the detail
that made me give in: I wasn't that reckless or
suicidal yet back in those days. I am thus, at
least in my own eyes, a minor sort of monster,
an entry-level monster, as salespeople call it
these days.

Ludmilla was more of a gerontophile than I
was a paedophile. She admitted to me one day
that she had had chronophilic tendencies since
early childhood. As a lover of textured Anglo-
Saxon novels, she claimed to relish my knotty,
parchment-like, sometimes eczema-ridden skin.

Ludmilla had also retained the sloppy habits
of children. She possessed all the attributes of
what I like to call frumpy charm. Her clothes
made her look like a female Charlie Chaplin:
her slacks (always too long), eaten to shreds
by the tread of her (equally worn-out) shoes,
her pullover often inadvertently turned back
to front (the label appearing in front on the

outside). And (I was on the point of forgetting), her very inviting, sometimes wide-open fly (I used to think this happened only to men), offering a view of the little boat pattern on her knickers. But there is no sublime-slovenly charm without a few additional touches: flow of knitted, scrubby hair (an ear sticking out monkey-style); fingers covered in ink as though stained by a blue cigarette; dreamy eyes, always clouded by the vapours of sleep.

When I saw her for the first time, at the back of one of my classrooms, she was already beaming, as if she had never stopped smiling since birth, as if smiling came to her more naturally than a neutral gaze at rest. A serenity without compare emanated from within her, a radiance that nothing could have troubled. Seeing her made me feel like a sunflower. Later, in fact, she nicknamed me Professor Sunflower, the character from the Tintin comics, for other, less glorious reasons (she used to say that like the comic strip figure, I was given to misunderstandings).

Curious as this may sound, our relations were thus purely visual to begin with. Even after our first lovemaking, our greatest pleasure lay in looking at each other without touching, with the same smile we had exchanged that first day, with the same radiant shyness.

What captivated me about her smile was its extraordinary presence. I have never felt such proximity in a stare. The people I had loved had always had something distant in their eyes. An unsurmountable gap whose cruelty I felt without fully realizing. Ludmilla's eye had not had the chance to retract, to withdraw into its socket. For the first time in my busy life, thanks to her, I also felt present, as though after a long absence.

Ludmilla didn't talk much. She didn't feel the need to. And so I didn't either. When she came to my place (our only refuge), I would open the door and we would gaze at each other at length, in the silence of the spring. Her smirk would make mine blossom. Our smiles stuck together felt like an erection of the lips, a turgidity we savoured. We would kiss in slow motion, without passion, tasting each second of voluptuous lip, the way you savour a ripe strawberry, the sun in the strawberry, the blood of the berry. Little by little, we would eat each other's faces. She would kiss my cheeks, I would lick her ear at length; she would suck my nose (which is particularly pleasant, regardless of what you might think); I would bite her neck. Our fevers were calm, without agitation or precipitation, as if we knew that time was of no consequence—something we were wrong about. It was as if, deep down, we were waiting for her to grow during the embrace, until she grew to be my age, my ripe soil making her flourish.

As a name for her, Ludmilla is perhaps too robust, now that I think of it. I'm going to go with a more delicate, ethereal name.

All in all, Camille had relatively little sexual appetite, and she found our infrequent lovemaking a source of pain. I'm not even sure she really felt any desire for me, something which bothered me from time to time. She was adamant that she did, and that without the pain she would often long to have me inside her. We contented ourselves with dry-humping and gazing deep into each other's eyes.

Our onanistic outbreaks cast me back to my teenage years, to a bygone, almost forgotten time when I would masturbate like mad, with the greatest dedication: in the swimming pool and the cinema, on my bike, on foot, on the back seat of my parents' car, in the field in front of the school at break time, and finally, so I wouldn't die of boredom there, in maths class.

This erotic friction allowed us much more freedom than coitus would have to choose our locations and our every position: discreetly in museums, mostly in photo exhibitions; less discreetly, in shops and on deserted street corners. Her mouth ajar, looking vaguely surprised like a child gazing at an oversized snail, she would take hold of my member to get a closer look.

But the most beautiful moments of this masturbatory liberty would occur in the more intimate sphere of the house. Three memories, all three haloed with roundness. I stroke her pubic area as she negligently bites into an apple. She fingers my glans, blowing huge bubble gum bubbles out of her slightly open mouth. She palms me, anointing my body with bubbles from the bubble bath, to the beat of the song being broadcast on the radio: "Friends First" by Georges Brassens.

Most of all, I was captivated by her animal-like spontaneity. She would hold my penis the way you hold a hot dog at a fair, with such casualness, such awkwardness, it used to bowl me over. She had no technique whatsoever. She would concentrate on eating her apple, or blowing her gum, her hand distractedly latched onto my member, as if dreamily pulling herself up the handrail on a flight of stairs.

At the start of the spring, I contracted a bad case of angina after an excursion to the Alps which we had undertaken, both naked, wearing nothing but our mountain boots. (As we say in France, "in April never shed a paedophile").

Bedridden, glued to my sheets by a fetid jam of fever and mucus, a peach stone lodged in my throat, I came very close to catching pneumonia. Camille would come and take care of me as soon as she was home from school. She would clean me off from head to foot, wipe the sweat off my brow, pamper me, plant suppositories between my butt cheeks with great skill and joy. In fact, she acquired such a taste for this latter activity, that when I no longer needed them she insisted on stuffing me with suppositories (two, three or four would go in when I was too weak to protest). She enjoyed this game so much I would let her get on with it most of the time without voicing any complaints.

We would look at each other like a mother smiling at her infant, without knowing who was playing the role of the mother, who the role of the infant. I would suck her breasts like I had never sucked since childhood. When she dragged her fingers through my hair as I sucked there at her nipple, my entire head felt like a glans under the strokes of a flesh comb. Every follicle felt titillated with micro-pleasure. In turn, she would suck at my chest, so hard and long that there were times when I felt like a wet nurse.

She sucked up the hidden femininity from deep inside me, drawing sensations out to the surface that most men repress. Hitched to my nipple, she would breathe femininity into my depths, rekindling in my breast all the femaleness I had relinquished in the womb.

That's when a completely unreal thing occurred. Something which, for the space of a few moments, gave us the very distinct feeling of finding ourselves in a Latin American novel in which strange and unrealistic things occur.

You're going to think that this is zany, grotesque and utterly fanciful. Your reactions will be understandable. And yet this is how it really happened.

One day, she had been sucking my tender nipple for over an hour (of the two of us, she was the one who practiced most diligently), when I saw to my greatest astonishment a fine streak of whitish liquid trickle down onto my belly. My first reaction was to think this was dribble, but the colour of the fluid was far too white to be saliva.

I shook Camille by the shoulder to make sure, as she had practically fallen asleep against my chest and seemed to be sucking in her sleep the way nurslings do. She opened her eyes and let a trickle of the same white liquid flow out between her lips. Suddenly wide awake, she burst out into a rapturous

"Oh, my God!"

"This isn't possible ..."

I fingered my chest, detecting a set of small lumps under my epidermis. There seemed to be hard nodules lodged around my areola, like a cluster of little pebbles under my skin.

"It tastes like sweet milk ...!"

"What are you talking about?"

"I swear to God! Can't you see it's milk?!

I read about that in a magazine, a scientific

review I found in the school library. Men are equipped with primitive lactation glands. It's well-known to scientists. Men can potentially produce milk for the survival of the species, in extreme circumstances. Anthropologists say that it has probably already occurred in times of famine. All you have to do is stimulate lactation and hey presto! You're not the first man to have achieved this. Some transmen already breastfeed, you know."

"Great. I feel entirely reassured ..."

"I wanted to see if it was possible. Which is why I sucked your nipple so much. Oh, come on! Don't look so crestfallen. You said so yourself the other day, we're all potentially women .... Man is a woman like any other."

When the evening came, I sought refuge and comfort in the Little Robert (a dictionary that is something of a soothing, sacred relic for French teachers). At the "milk" entry, it said: "white, opaque, highly nutritious liquid (rich in emulsified fat). UHT milk, long-life milk. Drink delicious milk. The milk of human kindness."

After this almost surreal discovery, I demanded to try it out on her too in the following days. Without balking, on the contrary, Camille agreed to have me suck her breasts at length as hard as I could. Two days later, I still hadn't managed to draw a drop. Nothing. At the end of the third day, when I had given up hope, I suddenly felt a liquid squirt into my mouth.

It had a taste I knew well, but it most definitely wasn't milk.

I got up to spit the contents out of my mouth.

My hand had a red stain on it.

I decided in the days that followed not to insist as much. The vision of her blood on my hand and her breast, on my lips and teeth, had disturbed us. It was a sign that sooner or later our relationship would be doomed. I quickly disposed of the omen down the sink.

After a week of gentle but persistent sucking, I finally obtained what we were looking for. A little pink at first, and then as white as white can be. From that day onwards, we vowed not to drink or eat anything other than our own milk and for over a month that's what we did, without cease.

It's hard to calculate just how many decil-itres we would swallow in any given day. Whatever it was, as soon as classes were over, we would breastfeed. The need to feed grew so urgent that we resorted to meeting in the school toilets and sometimes, on one or two occasions, in the classroom, after my Tuesday classes.

For the duration of the class, we would exchange greedy stares, our breasts pierced with pleasure.

As soon as the session came to a close, we would wait for the noise of pupils to recede from the corridor to indulge our dairy diet. Camille would lift my shirt in feverish haste and swoop in to suck my swollen teats, quenching her thirst with my milk-dispensing stones. I sometimes had to pull her painfully off her manger to satisfy my craving for nourishment, as there was more than just desire at stake.

We had both lost a few kilos with that diet, to the extent that I was often tormented by hunger whilst teaching, especially when I found her sitting there in front of me. I was sometimes given to nausea and mild spells of dizziness caused by inanition. My colleagues kept asking about my health, wondering why I no longer had lunch at the canteen.

When my turn finally came, by will or by force, I would slip my hands onto her midriff and push her shirt up over her flesh bubble breasts. My hunger was so intense, I feared they might burst.

I was astonished each time to find her chest remained so rotund and firmly resistant, despite my assaults. Camille's breasts didn't seem to be governed by the laws of gravity. As far as I remember, even the girls I used to go out with when I was her age weren't graced with breasts of that kind.

Day after day, Camille's bosoms were enough to quench all my thirsts. They sometimes seemed to have doubled in size. I practically didn't even miss penetrative sex. Kneading her bread dough, I sucked it to satiation, sometimes beyond. We swam in a sea of milk.

With time, we started to take more and more risks, until the day we heard a burst of muffled laughter from behind the door of room 412.

Struck by a lightning bolt of fear, we had rushed to put on our clothes, our hearts agitated like a hive fallen to the ground.

III

That's when Ophelia started to change, from one day to the next.

This third name is decidedly more in phase with the dark period in our story as Camille's blondness was beginning to be shaded with jasper-like hues. She started to sink day after day into the murky, troubled waters that had drowned Ophelia.

Speaking less and less, she kept her head down in class. Most of my pupils did nothing but stare at me, their faces devoid of kindness, their eyes dark with reproof. They obviously took me for some kind of pervert, an old lecher flushed out of his warren, a monster finally caught as he was breaking cover, ready to be subjected to the death blow and general opprobrium. In class, some of them refused to answer my questions. They glared at me coldly, a loaded rifle in their eyes.

From that day onwards, she started to sit at the back of the room, as far as possible from my desk. One day, as I was raising my eyes to start teaching, I saw that, contrary to her wont, she was wearing what, from a distance, looked vaguely like a lace choker.

But moving forward a little—declaiming a few paragraphs of *The Orgy, the Snow* by Patrick Grainville to accustom my pupils to the sound of baroque writing—I saw that it wasn't a necklace at all. What I had taken for a choker looked very much like a string of love bites, or marks of strangulation at regular intervals.

With feigned composure, still declaiming mechanically, I walked up the other side of the row where she was sitting and saw that the violet marks didn't go right around her neck.

On the other side of her neck were what looked strangely like a series of perfectly symmetrical, parallel scratch marks.

They looked like five bloody cuts, like a sort of burgundy-coloured barcode that had been inflicted on her in a high-tech concentration camp. As if she had been clawed in the neck by Thanatos. I wondered for an instant if it wasn't a tattoo, or my own hallucinations. I tried to question her with a look, but she refused obstinately to raise her head.

On Tuesday evening, she left the classroom, casting an overly-brief glance in my direction. It left me at once crushed and stricken. I couldn't understand her behaviour, this fresh batch of somatic reactions. I was afraid I had made her feel cornered, made her prey to some form of (self-)punishment. Had I pushed her into someone else's arms, hurt her or bruised her involuntarily in my dreams?

I feared I had disgusted her, pushed her away without wanting to. At the same time, I couldn't stop myself from feeling embittered by the strangeness of her behaviour. She was so different, so unlike her adolescent peers in so many respects.

I was powerless to do anything. I couldn't order her to come and have a word with me at the end of the lesson, I couldn't phone her place, even less appear on the doorstep of her family home. I decided to write to her, despite the risk that involved.

I should tell you that in the French state education system, the golden rule is this: insult each other, show (the utmost, deepest) contempt for one another, but avoid setting it down in writing.

It took me all night to compose my letter (being old-style romantics, we both loathed email). Two days later, by return post, I got the letter I had been waiting for. Always so calligraphic, imbued with candour and delicacy, her handwriting plunged me into a turmoil of emotions.

> *My little Sunflower,*
> *Forgive me, it's terrible. My pain is as*
> *deep as yours. I miss your milk so awfully*

*and am drowning in emptiness. My throat is
full of sand.*

*But whatever you do, I beg of you, don't
come near me anymore. Don't try to talk to
me. Believe me, there's more at stake than
just your job. My father knows about our
relationship (I know not by what traitor).
He wants to denounce you to the Board of
Education. I begged him on my knees not to
do anything of the kind. He banged the door
on his way out, but I think you are out of
danger for the time being.*

*Yesterday, he told me that if I see you
again, if I so much as utter a word to you, he
will kill you without thinking about it twice.
I know he means what he says and I know he
is capable of doing it. When we were living in
India, he stabbed a thief who had broken into
our house.*

*I beseech you, do not come near me. Don't
underestimate him. We must be patient.*

Ophelia

When I finished reading her letter, I broke
into tears. The situation seemed insoluble,
kidnapping and parricide being difficult to
accomplish, especially without incurring
punishment.

The days that followed drifted by like a
gluey tide. I stopped eating, drank only cow's

milk. I felt so weak I fell twice and had to stay in bed for I don't know how many days. I was tossed about by waves of nausea, incessant migraines.

Some high-ranking official must have taken an administrative measure as one morning I found the police at my door. I thought for an instant that they had come to carry me off to the police station, but to my surprise they only wanted to know if I was alright. They inquired politely, wanting to know the reason I wasn't coming to class, why I didn't answer my phone. I think my answers were barely coherent because they turned towards each other to exchange a look. I must have looked pretty poorly as one of the officers took a few steps back to call an ambulance.

After convalescing for a week, still on my meds, I tried to go back to school, obsessed as I was by my need to see Ophelia. When I finally entered the class I was supposed to have with her, I saw she was missing.

A giant emptiness sat there, enthroned on her chair. A gaping hole between two students, as if an enormous monster had bitten the class, taking a mouthful of pupil away from the seat of my feelings.

The unexpected emptiness threw me into a deep state of agitation. I couldn't collect my thoughts and found myself completely unable to start teaching. I knew I must on no account query her classmates about her absence, but I couldn't stop myself from asking in a tremulous, uncertain voice:

"Is Ophelia absent?"

No answer, then:

"Yeah, she's gone ..."

Knowing smiles, sidelong mocking stares.

"W-What do you mean?" I sputtered.

"She doesn't want you any more, sir!"

"Shut the fuck up, asshole!" yelled Mélanie from the other side of the room.

"Sir, she's left the country. Her father was posted to Bangkok."

"... Bangkok?"

"Yes, sir, in Thailand. He's going to be a consul there."

" ... Ok ... thanks ... Gwénola ... Right, then ... take out ... ah ... *Antigone*. We were looking at the second-last scene ... of the third act."

As the heroine says, I thought, the rest means nothing.

I taught the class in an extreme state of inner turmoil (outward turmoil too, I think, if my pupils' stares were anything to go by). I asked questions without listening to the answers. I sometimes even forgot the question I had asked. Anyway, the pupils were rather understanding in spite of everything and didn't disrupt the session, even when I stopped teaching, my eyes staring into space for I know not how many minutes.

I forced myself to come to class, though, as I knew that staying in bed would finish me off, and the void under my second-floor window enticed me almost as much as Ophelia's open mouth.

Her absence is death to me. I had been expecting at least a break-up letter, or another letter full of hope, but I'm still waiting for it. Ophelia disappeared with her father overnight, vanishing into thin air.

In the first days, I imagined myself going to the French embassy in Bangkok in the hope of finding her. I saw myself sinking into a laughable nightmare in a duel with Polonius in the damp heat of the tropics. I realized after a few hours of packing that my heart wasn't in it. It was pointless of course. I would just have ended my days in prison and no doubt have lost Ophelia's affection. We would have to wait two years before she came of age. I told myself that that was more than enough time for her to forget me in the arms of a young expatriate or a local heartthrob.

IV

The final days of the year trickle down on me like the last grains through the bulb of a sandglass. The anxiety-inducing thought of facing the void without a routine, no matter how boring, terrifies me. Here I am, a stray dog again at the age of fifty. No partner, no children. Another failed relationship to chalk up on the list of my accomplishments. One failure too many.

I attend the going-away party that my colleagues have organized for the trainee teachers who are to be exiled to Lille, Langres or Lamballe. Mr. Clog, the maths teacher, tells me he intends to carry out a very "pointed" visit to Lyon. He talks about his holidays as if they were a compass, stamping the ground with his foot, as always, to signify determination. I wish him the best of luck. He stamps the floorboards hard.

In the corridor, I spot Mr. Gift, the sports instructor, practically one-legged since his scuffle with a female pupil from Créteil. He

limps over, a radiant grin playing on his lips.
He asks what I intend to do during the holidays.
I tell him that I might write a novel, if I can find
a topic. Otherwise, I wouldn't mind engaging
the services of a hooker. He grins tensely,
displaying a row of beautiful, athletic teeth.
He's training for a triathlon.

At the exit, near the school administration
offices, the Principal and the (Vice) Principal
are negotiating with the Head of the French
section. They're already preparing next year's
schedules. They have the faith of true believers
in the mission and will work throughout the
vacation if necessary, until they drop dead. Mrs.
Prey, the section Head, collapsed a few days ago
(a fainting spell triggered by her educational
mission).

The Vice Principal is prepared to sell his
body in the name of Education (for the modest
sum of 11,57 euros for each rectoral penetration)
and the Principal (a potentially naughty woman
who proves weak in the face of propriety)
always walks as if the reputation of her school
was the precious Soissons vase in her hands. As
soon as she sees me, she tries to carry it out of
harm's way.

I see in the eyes of the Head that she has
heard of my latest indiscretions. She stares at
me in silence, a rat at bay, her snout curled up,
her fur bristling.

Like everywhere else, there are a certain

number of rats in the French national school system. Right at the top, you have the drowned rat, closely followed by the rectorate. Lower down in the sewers, floundering about in the educational muck, a whole array of haloed rats: the rat-race-running professorate. But as a recent study shows, teachers are useful to society, when they don't occur in too large numbers, as each teacher eats 250 grams of garbage a day on average, in other words close to 4000 kilos of trash in the space of a lifetime, an ecological solution for the planet that shouldn't be overlooked. It is therefore unadvised to sterilize them or make them eat poisoned bait in the form of anticoagulant drugs.

The summer holidays have come upon us. Massive as moons.

The bed is soiled when I wake. My shirts smell of curdled milk.

Yesterday, I tried to turn my eyes to the sun to burn out my retinas. I want to go blind so I won't have to encounter my image, so I won't have to see anyone or anything. But nothing avails. No matter how hard I try to keep my eyes open as I gaze at the sun, they end up closing with an intense sting. The sunflower gyrates.

I see Adam wandering around, lost, in my garden; his Eve dead, bitten by the snake.

It all seems so empty.

Standing round the house, the trees seem nothing more than prison furniture. Everything is stale, worn-out, put out. A paralysing fixity overcomes me. Since Ophelia's departure, my daily life has taken on an air of tragic, inexorable doom. Everything is static. I find myself on a large chessboard, the Hearses' tiled floor. The pawns are unable to move because they are fastened, rooted to the ground.

And thus I decide to let it all go to the dogs and neglect myself even more. I stop washing, I sleep fully dressed. I let my nails and hairs sprout. Over the course of a few weeks, my salt and pepper beard is seasoned with more dubious spices. A vague stink of vomit wafts up. My feet resemble the paws of a werewolf. The smell of my socks (the same pair for at least three weeks) reminds me of old, ailing Roquefort cheese. I'm reluctant to inspect the seat of my underpants too closely, but from my vantage point it looks like it's harbouring a sort of malodorous slug. I'm becoming a tramp in my own mansion.

And then one day, in desperation, I decide to frequent the local prostitutes (absolutely, Mr. Gift). I'm relieved to see that even for a paid consultation, my first impulse is to perform a few in-depth ablutions. I spend a whole hour under the shower, scrubbing away with a brush, dousing myself with shampoo. After the shower, under the repeated assaults of the hair dryer my beard begins to bounce back slowly but surely, plumy and light. It feels like I have feathers lining my jaw.

I trim the nails of my hands and feet, getting rid of the dead skin and all apparent callouses. After half an hour of care, my feet begin to look human again.

I don a new pair of underpants and a pair of fresh socks, a clean shirt and pants and hey presto. I'm presentable.

Surfing the Web for the first time this month, I acquaint myself with the milieu through the promotional porn sites. To begin with, to purge myself of the jealousy that's been eating away at me at the thought of Ophelia in the arms of a young man with drop-dead looks, I decide to get drunk on alluring young pussy.

I have them one by one on Ophelia's bed to desacralize it as far as I can.

When evening falls, I shed a few tears on the soiled surface of her pillow.

When after a few days of frenetic debauchery, guilt starts to set in, I decide to punish myself for these shameful infidelities. I get in touch with the ugliest hookers, the most demolished ones, the most chubby-cheeked and spotty, those that look the sickest.

Having an orgasm in such conditions is a tight-rope walker's feat, almost a spiritual quest. But as I engage in sexual congress with these poor, sad-faced ladies, I surprise myself

by finding great arousal in the thousand imper-
fections of the human frame. And I am not just
talking of love handles bulging out of jeans, but
varicose veins, warts, stretch marks, slumped
bellies, bed sores, scoria, flaccid, sagging,
wrinkled flesh, over-hairy, spiky, grainy, cellu-
lite-covered thighs, bloated, greasy, sticky lips
smeared with lipstick, pudgy fingers, oakum,
greasy hair, red and black spots as large as
ticks, misshapen jug-ears, asymmetrical, carti-
laginous nostrils, Botox exoskeletons, sewn
up, patched up breasts, bursting like silicone
popcorn, and I spare you the details that could
offend your sensibility.

My first experience of orgasmic ugliness is a
trial by fire.

In the event, the apparent beauty of my first
olden street walker meets my former standards
of acceptability. Her face is well proportioned,
her breasts relatively prominent, curvaceous and
appealing, but when she peels off her skin-tight
pants, I discover that her legs are covered in
varicose veins, each more ornamental and finely
wrought than the last. Blue and violet lightning
forks and flashes, hither and thither, here and
there, veining the surface beneath her skin.

I force myself to contemplate the tempest in
these veinlets, at first to expiate my sins through
self-punishment, but in the later reaches to
push myself, surprisingly, to a sudden rush of
ecstasy.

It's astounding what you can accomplish
with great concentration, a relativist philosophy
of aesthetics and a good dose of autosuggestion.
Despite the alternative beauty of her marbled
skin, however, I leave more spunk than sparks
between her legs.

With lowered eyes, we flash a smile at
each other when parting. I manage to find her
touching without having to force myself. She
seems to find me vaguely friendly. She treats
me to a slightly timid smile. I may be the first to
appreciate the scribbles on her skin.

It's exalting to realize so late (but not too
late) that sex can be so democratic, that it has a
capacity to transcend conventions and transform
time's humiliations into something sublime.

Sex has aesthetic virtues: on its own, it is
capable of transforming the way we perceive
things. Under its goodly influence, even
ugliness can be transmuted. I find the proof
of this in my second encounter with a lady of
the night who also happens to be old enough
to be a grandmother of the night. I should tell
you I have always savoured the presence of my
foremothers, even when they stopped me from
getting up to mischief.

I am therefore well equipped to find the
experience if not a draught of pure pleasure
than at least riveting.

And yet, nothing predisposes me to find the
old-time prostitute who presents herself at my

door that day in any way alluring. The poor
woman is so worn out and decrepit that I'm
tempted to ask her age, but politeness is of the
essence even, or perhaps especially, in this kind
of situation. You can rent a body at a charge,
but it doesn't give you access to the intimacy of
someone's psyche.

What surprises me this time is not my lack
of disgust, but the realization that my maypole
is erect without direct stimulation. It's as stiff,
if not more so, than when I faced my beautiful
bachelorette. Within a short lapse of time, I've
spanned the range of generations, from magnif-
icent maiden to village crone.

Despite my original inclinations, I find
myself becoming a gerontophile, as if I was
suddenly in Ophelia's shoes, as if I could
suddenly feel what she felt. Gerontophilia also
stems from a kind of nostalgia. It awakens our
memories of grandmothers, of our very first
contacts with ancient grease.

And thus I find myself mesmerized in front
of this naked, hoary, old lady, nailed in the air
by my own member. My organ nods like a bird
on the lookout.

The grandmother of the night looks at me,
a tranquil expression in her eyes, as if the
spectacle of my erection is nothing special. I am
thus not the first to find her arousing, despite
her late years.

When I settle down on top of her, the tactile

sensation comes as an even greater surprise. The comfort of some old folks is beyond compare.

Lying down on her body makes me feel like I am sinking into a huge hunk of bread dough that's still warm, soft and subtly sticky. Her fluffy skin is more than elastic. It's like puffy bubble gum. Plunging my wagtail into the depths of her flesh, I discover that her genitals are soft as the inside of marzipan-stuffed pastry in unctuous deliquescence. I nuzzle the tender sticky crumb of her neck. It harbours a strong scent of old yeast in the summer heatwave.

Kneading the dough of her skin between my hips, I stuff the whole of my scrotum into the mixture. Unable to read the thoughts that lie there to be deciphered in my unfortunate companion's eyes, I find her suddenly moving.

I don't even have to lay hold of her breasts to reach ecstasy. A surge of pleasure suddenly floods through my pelvis. Convulsing briefly on top of her, I bury my face in the hollow of her shoulder. The puffy coating of her flesh muffles my lowing.

When after a few minutes I withdraw (leaving behind me a little streak of custard), a flap of her skin peels off my thigh like a pancake. I swear I do not jeer when I say that the whole experience comes close to the sublime.

Despite these most promising beginnings (a good dozen ravaged prostitutes follow in her wake), the last of these poor women is so spent and wooden that I am forced to leave before she finishes her service.

When her much younger and energetic pimp catches up with me on the stairs, I let myself be beaten up as if it was happening to someone else. Feeling as guilty as he is, I fail to muster the strength to report him.

The face that now looks out at me from the mirror is shaggy, over-bearded. I'm swollen, slashed, striated, splintered, wrinkled, exhausted, reddened, made ugly. Barely recognizable. Fairly discreet up to now, my middle-aged wrinkles avail of the opportunity to furrow my face with micro-puckering. I feel a kind of landslide in my skin.

Strange to say, this affords me some relief. My new face has the advantage of shaking up the motionless prison-like enclosure that surrounds me. Something to be grateful for. And tending my sores has given me something to do. I feel vaguely like a wounded warrior battling on. War is of course absurd but at least things happen in it. Only my taste for tragi-comedy keeps me from committing suicide. I'm fully aware that lacerating my soul is a way to avoid slashing my veins. Whatever.

V

To give solitude the slip the other day I told my neighbour I would like to go for a swim in his company. Despite his galloping senility, due in part to his very advanced years (he's over a hundred), Mr. Hearse goes to the swimming pool every day.

My guess is that you can count the number of metres he swims with the fingers on your hands and that his swimming doesn't therefore contribute much to his fitness, but it's an activity that at least allows him some reprieve from Mrs. Hearse's incessant natter for over an hour.

In any case, at the end of our swimming session, in the showers next to the changing rooms, Mr. Hearse's body appeared in a suddenly poignant light. That I should perceive it so is no doubt due to my recent intercourse. Touched, even moved, by the gauche stiffness of this broken being, I was unexpectedly impelled to lay my hand on the hairy skin of his skeletal shoulder.

The poor man even had trouble washing. He reminded me of one of those albino fish whose bones you can see through the translucent flesh.

He was pleased to accept my offer to help him so I took the bar of soap from his long bony fingers and soaped him down from head to foot, without forgetting to lather his armpits, the back of his neck and his diaphanous ears. I let the soap slide along his gaunt, long-haired hips, going down on his skinny calves and in between his arthritis-bent toes.

I noticed while doing this that one of his testicles was missing. I figured he must have had a kind of operation to have it more or less surgically removed. I say "a kind of" because the remaining skin on his scrotum seemed to have been burned and awkwardly sewn up a long time ago.

Whatever the case, within hardly a few minutes, he seemed regenerated, covered in a froth of opalescent bubbles. In the shimmering light, he seemed almost handsome, as though revitalized, strewn with angel feathers, lathered in beautiful seraphic bubbles.

I slid the soap over his translucent skin to his inner thighs. He quivered a little when I touched him there and laid a trembling hand against the tiling of the shower wall.

Under the foam, his circumcised member seemed no more wrinkled or ravaged than mine. Circumcision even added a touch of juvenile candour to his organ. Gently, I soaped between his legs, taking care not to scrub the remains of his scrotum too vigorously. I proceeded to place the bar of soap on the floor, casting him a questioning look.

Looking timid and earnest, he returned my stare, nodding encouragement: and so I took his bubbled shaft between my hands and started to shuttle back and forth, slowly at first, then increasing the pace.

I was surprised to discover that his member was far from defunct. Within barely a few seconds, his glans stood fully erect, rosy and very solid, crowned with a myriad of miniature soap bubbles. I got up next to him and masturbated him under the shower, casting my mind back to Ophelia at regular intervals, feeling almost appeased.

I had never tried this kind of thing before. Even as a teen, I hadn't been tempted to ogle other people's testicles. The bodies of my showering classmates at the gymnasium were of no more interest to me than white and brown slugs. And yet I must admit that caressing that old branch of flesh felt somewhat arousing.

Thinking back, though, I realize that eroticism was not foremost in my mind that day. Pulling back and forth, I marvelled more at the fact that I was palming the vital member of Mr. Hearse, my hundred-year-old neighbour with a testicle in the grave.

It was a bit like masturbating death. An allegorical experience, in a way. It seemed mind-boggling, almost unthinkable.

As my amazement faded a little, I caught myself thinking that I had at hand the phallus of a certified inspector. You might say I was holding the penis of the Board of Education between my fingers. It was a realization that seemed fraught with responsibility.

Mr. Hearse suddenly let out a weak groan and the Board of Education's sperm slowly slithered down over my hand like a streak of enriched, bluish milk.

Only as he was getting dressed (as in a slow-motion film) did I catch him tying a necklace with a Star of David around his neck. Seeing my scrutiny, he slowly turned his back and tried as best he could to hide the pendant under his shirt, as though suddenly afraid of being recognized.

He started to move in a somewhat agitated manner, avoiding my gaze another two or three times after that before recovering a degree of tranquillity. I wondered what might have happened under the Nazi occupation of France for him to react in this way, but on the spur of the moment I shied away from asking any questions on the subject. He looked so modest and stricken all of a sudden. It was particularly strange after what had just happened between us.

Today, that memorable moment in my life (since I've become disturbed, at least) seems utterly unreal. I don't see how I could have behaved out of character. Having slept very little, I wondered if the incident had actually taken place. Perceiving no difference in Mr. Hearse's expression, I was reluctant to mention it. It was possible he had already forgotten. In any case, he didn't look embarrassed in the least, on the contrary. I've come to the conclusion I must have dreamt it.

In the days that followed, I decided to spend a few days in Paris to try to get my mind off things, immersing myself in bookshops and museums. I paid a visit to the Musée du Quai Branly, the Musée Bourdelle, the Musée Pompidou, the Musée Moreau and the Musée d'Orsay.

When I returned, Mr. Hearse was dead.

I attended his funeral next to Mrs. Hearse who was shattered, in tears. She had even lost the faculty of speech. I realized I had some affection for her too, after all. I surprised myself by taking her in my arms.

A few weeks went by, and then one day Mrs. Hearse confided that she couldn't stand living in the house in which her husband had lived beside her for so many years. She had decided to sell the house and asked me if I wanted to buy it at a very reasonable price. She knew of course that the house had belonged to my great-grandfather back in the old days and that he had had to give it up for lack of money. He had always regretted losing the house in which his mother had been born and had always longed to buy it back. As a well-endowed heir, I offered to give Mrs. Hearse an extra fifty thousand euros on top of the price she was asking. She was very touched by the gesture and finally accepted.

Leaving for her retirement home after having moved some of her furniture, she confided that she didn't want to encumber her new dwelling place. She suggested I avail of the belongings she would leave behind. I was to keep what I liked and throw out the rest. She had neither the courage nor the strength to go and rummage in the attic among Mr. Hearse's old stuff. She enjoined me to empty it, if I didn't mind too much. In view of her bereavement, I agreed to deal with the drudgery.

The Letter

VI

I am now in the kitchen of this little sixty-square-metre house. The walls oppress me already. I'm trying to imagine the birth of my great-great-grandmother on my father's side in this place. I do my best to be mindful of my great-grandfather and the joy he would have felt at the idea of reclaiming his old family house.

I think of Ophelia, Polonius, love and death.

I get up from Mr. Hearse's armchair and put on the new slippers his wife bought him only a few weeks ago. We have exactly the same shoe size. I drag the slippers to the sitting room, contemplating the austerity of the walls around me, the greyness of the tiled floor so grid-like I start to sink into the doldrums. What an idiotic idea to buy the Hearses' house.

I venture to the bedroom where their marital bed stands. I lie in the middle of the bed, my fingers entwined on my chest like a recumbent statue.

I turn my eyes to the ceiling, and instead of drowning my thoughts in the white glare of the paint, I notice the fine outline of a square cut into the ceiling. White on White. It must be the hatch that leads to the attic.

I experience a slight jolt of curiosity that makes my spirits bounce back. I have always loved attics. They're so mysterious, so dark and cavernous. There's such a fantastic smell of darkness in them. Such a soft layer of downy ancestral dust.

Promptly restored to life, I stand up on the bed and push the trapdoor upwards with the tip of my middle finger. It gives without an effort, opening a black hole in the ceiling. I push the white square to the side of the opening.

Limbering towards the hole, I catch it with my two hands and pull myself up into the mouth of the ceiling. Passing through the threshold, I am given the sensation, for an instant, that I'm passing through the looking-glass.

Up in the attic, the air is dry. I can't see much and there doesn't seem to be a light switch anywhere. When I venture across the floorboards, my foot encounters what seems to be a series of cardboard boxes. Three boxes in all, a chandelier, a pair of size 10 ice-skates, an antiquated world map and a few leathery old books. I lay hold of these objects along with the boxes and let them drop one by one onto the bed before dropping down through the hole in a snow flurry of dust.

Heartened by my findings, I start to explore the boxes straightaway. The first one, the weightiest one, contains a large quantity of papers and stapled documents. As far as I can see, they're official papers, inspection reports, couched in the approved academic style. The hackneyed turns of phrase are there, all neatly aligned in a row in the appointed place. Contrary to what I was expecting, though, the reports are for the most part full of praise and those that bear some reservations are written with a lot of tact and nuance. Well done, Mr. Inspector, you were an enlightened photocopier. I see you will decidedly always surprise me.

I also find a few documents in English, a language he seems to master with great ease, as far as my somewhat limited knowledge allows me to judge. Looking at some of the reports, I see it's actually one of the subjects he used to inspect. Oh, well, nothing to get excited about there; I'll use them to light a nice bonfire. I'll relish burning the pages one after the other. Better still, I'll fold them into paper planes and send them out the window of the second floor of my main abode, instead of throwing myself out.

The second box is more interesting. It contains a few literary works, some of them all dog-eared. Others are bound hardbacks, first editions, *The Devil in the Flesh* by Raymond Radiguet, and (oh joy!) one of the first twenty copies of *Tiresias: the Secret Writings* by Marcel Jouhandeau. I have in my hands one of the first copies of the work, published back in those days under the cloak of secrecy. I can scarcely believe my eyes. There, I'm almost in a good mood. I feel a slight tremor of excitement in my bosom.

There's also a less glorious paperback of *Tiresias's Breasts*, Gérard Bessette's *Not For Every Eye*, *The Memoirs of Jean Marais* by Jean Marais and *Lady Chatterley's Lover* in both French and English (I understand now why Mr. Hearse's eyesight was so weak after that many hours spent reading with a flashlight in the darkness of the attic while Mrs. Hearse was enjoying her daily nap).

I savour the precious Jouhandeau in my hands, telling myself that it's highly likely the author palmed the copy himself ...

The third box is longer but a good deal lighter. This one contains a virgin wool turtleneck sweater (the itchy kind), a colonial hat, a suede-covered notebook full of crabbed handwritten notes, a well-sharpened cane-sword decorated with art deco motifs (I'll have to give it back to Mrs. Hearse—it must be worth a pretty sum), and a wooden casket about forty centimetres long and thirty deep. I put the colonial hat on my head and try to find something with which to open the box. The key, though, is nowhere to be found in any of the cardboard boxes.

I carry the mysterious parallelepiped casket off through the house in search of a substitute key. What precious treasure have you been stashing away, Mr. Hearse? A revolver, an aspirin tube filled with Louis d'or coins, love letters from your youth that Mrs. Hearse would have been delighted to burn, a coprolite fossil, a moulded silicone vibrator, the labia of the Education board? I have a gut feeling that the contents of this casket is going to titillate me.

I manage to spring open the cover of the casket thanks to a fork left in the kitchen sink. The first thing I lay eyes on is a length of yellowy-orange watered fabric that's particularly silky to the touch. It doesn't look like the kind of material that's sold in Europe. Is this a table cloth, a bedspread or some kind of exotic cape? One of the four corners of the fabric is torn in a very irregular manner.

Under the textile lies another length of light beige cotton fabric. It's tied around a few objects that you can feel through the bundle of coarse cotton. Chipping my nails, I finally manage to open the tight knot and empty the box out onto the table. Bits of torn paper flutter to the floor as soon as I do this. I catch one in my hand as it flutters down.

Come
9 o'clock
impossible
your

Come 9 o'clock impossible your!

On my word, Mr. Cuckold, this is part of an invitation letter! And that drawing of lips and the nose next to "come" is very compromising!

There's no doubt about it, what I have here is an old love letter. But there's only a part of the first letter of the woman's Christian name: your T or your J? I pick up one of the fallen shreds and read what looks like "rnude" or "tunude".

Examining it closely, I realize it could be the French word "timide". Rummaging through the various objects cluttering the table, I notice briefly that they look rather unusual and pick out another yellowed fragment of the letter.

There appears to be something like the drawn outline of a nose at the top of the fragment and what looks like a signature: "Tean Coci". Your cuckold? Your coccyx? Your coconut? Then a hesitant, but ascending line, not a heart or a flower: a star.

I ferret out another epistolary fragment from the jumble and come across Cuckold's full address:

MADELEINE PALACE-HOTEL
35, PLACE DE LA MADELEINE
1, RUE TRONCHET
PARIS

Téléphone : GUTENBERG 29 41
C. DENEUX, PROP

The brevity of the telephone number and the associated name indicate it's definitely not a recent letter. Surmising that an extra one or two digits are added every ten years, that brings us at least as far back as the 1940s. Mr. Hearse must have been a dashing young man in those days.

This time, I happen upon another strip of letter which floors me.

Unbelievable. Simply incredible. Adding the third piece to the one I have in my hand, I get a name that is, to say the least, unexpected.

A letter of invitation penned by Jean Cocteau himself! I can scarcely credit what I'm seeing. In a flurry, I gather the fallen bits of paper to assemble the following letter:

MADELEINE PALACE-HOTEL
35, PLACE DE LA MADELEINE
1, RUE TRONCHET
PARIS

Téléphone : GUTENBERG 29 41
C. DENEUX, PROP

Dear little one

Don't be timid—I swear I'm not intimidating and we are old acquaintances. Come Sunday Evening at 9. If the evening is impossible, give me a ring.

Your
Jean Cocteau

Good old Mr. Hearse ... I must say he's impressed me this time. I was definitely wrong to take him for a bore. This is pretty admirable stuff for a supposedly shy person. I try to imagine Mr. Hearse being timid. Now that I think about it, behind the veil of near-senility you could sense his embarrassment, a certain social awkwardness, even a slight speech impediment.

In any case, the portrait of Mr. Hearse that's scribbled on the letter is particularly well executed, especially for a sketch drawn from memory: his almost Grecian profile, with that characteristic bump on the nose, a nose so large it came close to being ungainly. The oval forehead which, seen frontally, so touchingly evoked the shape of an overlarge egg. He wasn't exactly what you would call breathtakingly beautiful, but he must have been handsome enough to take Jean Cocteau's fancy. As Cocteau used to say, youth must have stood in for beauty.

I imagine Mr. Hearse was touched that such an eminent man went to the trouble of drawing his profile from memory on an invitation.

I wonder if Mr. Hearse was married at the time he received the missive, but there's no way of checking that detail. The envelope that went with the letter is nowhere to be found.

Locking the door of the little house as if I was turning the key in a jewel box, I hurry over

to compare the drawing with the ones I have
at home in a book of Jean Cocteau illustrations.
I'm in such a state of excitement that the slight
sense of shame I feel at rifling through someone
else's life doesn't manage to trouble me. Feeling
scarcely more guilt than a kid shoplifting
a sheet of paper in a superstore, I put my
conscience quickly to sleep, telling myself that
in any case Mrs. Hearse would hardly receive
this missive with the most heartfelt alacrity.

Having conscientiously stuck the letter back
together again on a sheet of paper, I place it
next to the book of drawings which I think quite
faithfully informs me of the letter's approximate
date of composition.

What's certain, in any case, is that the
drawing doesn't belong to the author's first
works. The *Potomak* and other *Eugène* drawings
of his youth are diametrically opposed, in
stylistic terms. Thanks to the star, the seal
appended to a great number of Cocteau's works,
I've determined a time bracket that spans the
decade from 1930 to 1940.

The writer's first stars are well outlined and
confidently executed. They seem to say "here
I am, Jean Cocteau, a rising star, I share Jesus
Christ's initials". They also display a need to
remain simple, an entertainer, still connected
to childhood, availing all the while of a certain
cosmic sweep: eternal return, Cocteau forever.
The little dot in the middle of the star suggests a

willingness to complicate: it seems to assert that
this is no ordinary star. An enigmatic dotted
star, eluding analysis.

In the years before the war, the star in his
drawings is subjected to a number of mutations.
It falls apart, swells up again, gathering itself
in, blackening itself against its own mass. Is the
tremendous weight of the war bearing down on
the Star of Bethlehem? Does this collapse reflect
Cocteau's fear of being taken for a Jew under
Germany's occupation of France? His first stars
are not that far removed from the Star of David.
Whatever the case may be, the stars that emerge
on his drawings in the 1950s and 60s are in
general no longer more than squished spiders,
or dismantled into the shape of a straight-
forward cross.

The eyes are what strike me the most in
these drawings. Ultimately, you could say that
Cocteau did for the eye what Egon Schiele did
for the navel. In fact, Cocteau's eyes are a little
like belly buttons.

Most of the time, his irises are empty orbs,
sometimes they're black pearls set in the casket
of the eyelids; elsewhere, they float free in orbit.
In the more loosely-executed drawings, to which
the drawing in the letter belongs, the eye is
sliced by the line of the eyelid. These crossed
out stares seem to be granted long-sighted
vision. The eye is transformed into a treble clef
that announces the musical stave of the face.

Having placed this missing page in
Cocteau's oeuvre in my book, I go back all
excited to the remarkable little house of dearly
departed Mr. Hearse. My exaltation has made
me forget the other objects in the casket; even
the Jouhandeau book now seems pale by
comparison.

The box contains some pretty bizarre objects.
The first things I come upon are a little ivory
hand, a sort of dried up litchi that looks discon-
certingly like an eye gazing straight at me, as
well as four small, quite distinctive creatures.

The first creature I lay eyes on vaguely
resembles the wingless trunk of a dragonfly.
The little streamlined body is dry and brittle. It
grates a little, crumbling to ashes between my
fingers.

Under the dragonfly is a glass box which
contains the remains of a butterfly. One of its
electric blue wings is in shreds. What's left
of the body is pinned to a piece of yellowed
cardboard.

The third creature is actually just a fragment
of an animal. It looks like the tail of a snake.
There's still a slight whiff of rot wafting around
it.

The fourth animal looks like a ball of hair no
larger than a toenail. Its smallness is fascinating.
I free an infinitely small face with a set of fangs
fine as needles from where they are concealed in
the fur. The thing looks like a Lilliputian mouse.

Fascinated by this bunch of souvenirs, I lay them delicately out one by one on the table like museum exhibits from another planet. I have a vague feeling that all these objects are somehow bound together by a connecting thread that's invisible to the naked eye. There may well be a very coherent story behind this little heterogeneous collection.

The suede notebook seems to be some kind of diary. Maybe I'll find a few explanations in that. Who knows, there might even be material in there I could use for a novel. Perhaps I'll be able to bury my vacant soul in the rubble of words.

Stuck to the last page of the notebook is a yellow envelope containing the photograph of a man covered in medals. He looks like an Asian king or a warlord. Someone has drawn doodles on his face leaving a whole series of little parodic adjustments in the most typical schoolboy style. At the back of the photo, I find these words scribbled in haste: "post the letter of the young girl on the quay—Camille".

Seeing this name throws me instantly into a state of disarray. It dunks my head straight back into its torments after only a few minutes of respite. The discovery of Mr. Hearse's treasure had allowed me to forget all detrimental thoughts for a few moments. Here they are back with a vengeance, popping out like a jack in the box striking me squarely in the face.

With a surge of emotion, I make a grab for Hearse's cane-sword. I feel like tearing everything apart, like lacerating the wallpaper. I have a gut feeling that before this story is over someone will be impaled on its tip. So here's the murder weapon. The murderer and the victim remain to be found.

The Young Snow Man

VII

Thick, shredded snowflakes flutter down from the sky. Soft, mushy snow. The gaslights all around are muffled by the wadding of the snow, looking as if they are about to be quenched from one moment to the next, like candles snuffed out.

There was snow that night. It had been falling since the day before and naturally set another scene. The city was receding through the ages; vanished from the comfortable soil, it seemed as if the snow had fallen and piled up in drifts nowhere else but there.

It rests on the footpaths as if dirtied by night. Grey snow, almost black. My leather ankle boots tread mechanically on the cold carpet of flakes. I'm late but unable to hurry. The top half of my body won't allow me.

Only my feet and my legs rise to the call of duty. They move by rote, as if drawn by puppet strings. The ankle boots stop. They stop moving forward. I am not moving.

All around me, everything is just as still, apart from this shower of flakes.

In a garden that's hardly larger than a few strides, a snowman gives me a cold stare with stony eyes. His carrot nose seems to mock me, turning the scene into a dismal, grim circus. He's wearing the same bowler hat as I am.

I tip my hat to him with a grand, sardonic gesture.

There isn't a cat in sight. Even the taxis have stayed in their garages. I haven't seen a single one of them since I left my doorstep. In any case, I don't want to be on time and even less early. I don't even want to get there at all. And yet my heartbeat is racing, banging away in my chest like a shoe. My brain seems to have decided against moving forward, but my indomitable heart carries on. It knows that the rest of me will follow inevitably. It knows that sooner or later I will be forced to give in. It keeps time to the rhythm of the music, rising up to *vivace*, regardless of the fact that I'd like to finish this stretch of road *caminando*.

The gaslights keep displacing my shadow. As soon as I've trampled it, my shadow spills out in front of me again: a slick of oil that oozes out of a hole in my soles.

What is he going to think of me if I can't get a word out, if the words stick in my throat as they so often do in public? That slipknot of muscles that chokes my throat up like a noose.

*He opens his mouth: "Darg..."; the moment
he utters the word, the snowball hits his mouth,
penetrating it, paralysing his teeth. He has just
enough time to notice someone laughing. Beside the
laugh, in the midst of his henchmen, Dargelos rises
up, his cheeks flaming, his hair in disarray, finishing
off his grand gesture.*

I know it by heart. And I'm stuck with
the feeling that it's all I can say. As if I learned
to speak with it, as if I was nursed by it
throughout my childhood. A saint's book, a
breast-book, a baby-bottle of a book.

There you go, you see. You're managing,
you'll be able to talk to him, you'll know how to
earn his respect. It's said he has a fondness for
wordplay.

It'll be enough to assert yourself, show
him that you're not just a young man without
substance.

"Hearse! Hearse! Do you want us to drive
you to the graveyard? Hey, egghead! We're
talking to you."

The bastards. I hate them.

I feel their feet on my face, on my throat, my
chest and my belly. My fear of others is their
fault.

Which is why you're going to go and
confront them, crush them, pummel them to a
paste.

I start running to our meeting place. My

ankle boots slap the ground, rasping against the snow. I'm engaged in a running race against my own pulse.

Slipping on the road, I come to a spread-eagled stop after a spectacular tumble.

Nothing broken, despite the fact that I bounced off my head. There's even snow in my neck and in my socks. My hat is completely crushed. I'm consumed with shame at the idea of presenting myself in this state in front of the man I so admire.

Enough fussing. Let us go anyway.

Patted down, smoothed over, combed and re-hatted, I find myself in front of the address mentioned in the letter: 1 rue Tronchet, le Madeleine Palace-Hôtel.

I'm a bit taken aback by the state of the hotel. I had imagined it was going to look splendid; what lies before me is a modest-looking boarding house. As for my heart, it's beating out the last bars of a syncopated symphony.

I go into the entrance hall, despite myself.

At the reception, I ask in a faltering voice for the number of Mr. Jean Cocteau's room. I'm told with a sardonic smile that it's on the last floor but that the lift is on the blink. I'm out of luck.

Trembling, I pull myself up the banister, climbing the interminable staircase, one step at a time, dropping a piece of myself at every step.

When I finally get to Mr. Cocteau's daunting door, I'm no more than a black coat topped with a hat. Under my flattened bowler the remains of a human being are pooling. No longer really me. My brow is burning, my chest beating wildly. My fist still hesitates a few millimetres from the door.

Although I haven't decided it, my fist is trembling so much that my knuckles start to knock at the door.

Something hits him straight in the chest. A dark knock. A marble punch. A statue's crushing blow. His head s-

"H-Hello, Monsieur ... good-good evening, I mean."

"Good evening, good evening! Do come in, my dear friend! You must be freezing! Come in quickly and sit by the heater."

He's even more elegant than the other day, even more distinguished looking. His calm literary voice velvety with fellow-feeling.

He sits me down in an armchair next to a radiator turned on full blast. The moment I come into contact with the heating device, a wave of tingles pours an ant-pile over my head.

Retrieving a handful of sticky ants from my forehead, I mop my hand on my overcoat.

"My dear little one, would you care for a cup of tea?"

"Uh ..."

"I'll bring it over! Relax. Make yourself
at home. This is your place, my little one.
Whatever you do, don't feel embarrassed."

I pull another handful of burning ants off
the nape of my neck and smear them discreetly
against the fabric of my trousers.

I hear his voice crying from the kitchenette:

"I'm delighted you're here! I was afraid you
wouldn't come!"

The hot ants keep multiplying, running
along my arms and thighs. I stir up the ant-heap
in my hair with my fingers.

"Do take off your coat, my dear friend, it
isn't really that cold."

"Yes ..."

"Are you not feeling well? You look all
congested."

"No ... not ... I ... it's ... the ... cold."

"My, my, you're really sensitive to the cold.
Do place your hands on the radiator!"

"N-no. I mean ... the heat. It's ... the heat."

"Oh, that makes more sense! You're all
red. My goodness, let me take your coat. I'll
turn off the radiator. You should have told me.
Please excuse the mess, I'm all worked up at
the moment trying to write an article so critics
are ready to receive my new play. I'm finding
it devilishly hard to come up with an apologia
that will be received as I intend it to be."

"*The Terrible Pa-Parents?*"

"No, no, that play hasn't been conceived yet.

I'll write it in ten years. I'm talking about *The Infernal Machine*."

"Oh, yes, I've heard of it ..."

"You have? How delightful. I feel a play can only be written by a natural born dramatist— in other words, probably by someone who's an actor, most definitely by a stage director. The play itself must impose its own staging. It should unfold according to rules that are as strict as a set of chess rules and contain an implacable pantomime. It has to be a spectacle in which the eye, the ear, the heart, the soul, the mind and other less official senses must also be satisfied. By 'less official senses' I mean a kind of thirst for mystery, a desire for the unknown that almost all men experience, though they deny it and claim to seek a mere form of relaxation, a strange kind of relaxation that entails not displaying one's dirty linen ... Anyway, I must be bothering you with my palaver. You told me you write."

"Oh, no. It's just—scribbling ..."

"You're being modest, no doubt. I like that. Your shyness shows you're a sensitive soul. I hope you'll show me your work?"

"I won't be able to. My-My writing isn't worthy of you, Monsieur Cocteau."

"Jean! Jean. Call me Jean. Can I also call you by your first name? Remind me of your Christian name."

"Tho-Thomas."

"Totomas?"

"Nno, Tho-mmmas."

"Thomas! A Biblical name, as well as being one of my characters. You stand for doubt, lack of faith, existential crisis ... In fact, I see all these characteristics within you. Am I mistaken?"

"Uh, no, you mu-must be right."

"I knew it! You just have a lack of self-confidence. You know, I was myself shy back in the old days. It disappears with age. At the age of around nineteen, you shed it like a moult and then you forget you ever had it. What age are you now?"

"Nin-nineteen..."

He places a judicious index finger on his freshly-shaven cheek.

"I see, well around that age. It won't persist very long. We'll cure you of that! You know what? I'm going to commit to getting rid of your hang up."

"I'm very tou-touched by your ... concern. I don't want to be an imposition ..."

"Hogwash! I take a keen interest in you, young man. I'm very fond of your family. I'll be your guardian angel."

"Angel Heurtebise," I say, in a suddenly high-pitched voice.

"Ha! You see! You're changing already! I see your literary yearnings. You said as much in your letter. Right then, how are we going

to go about this? Let's see, let's see ... I think
I'm going to start by introducing you to Pablo
Picasso."

"Picasso! My God, that would be worse ..."

"Worse than me? We'll try that another time,
then. We could go and see Gide, but that might
be a bit premature. He's a bit stiff. So is Jouvet.
Proust is dead. Erik Satie is too. Perhaps Coco
Chanel might do the trick, or the poet Max
Jacob. We'll see how that goes. In any case, it is
to me that you have presented yourself. You're
in luck. I'm going to take good care of you.
We're going to proceed in a systematic way. I'm
not one of those Freudians, but I think I know
enough about the hardships of life to come to
your assistance. It seems to me that to allay
social anxiety, you have to dive into society.
Just as arachnophobes need to be touched by
spiders, you will have to surround yourself with
people. And I know some pretty large spiders!
How does that sound?! Tell me, how is your
mother? Your father was such a good-natured
man, poor soul."

The ants teem and intertwine with the
spiders.

"She's doing quite well, thank you."

"I'm happy to hear it. Your mother is a very
courageous woman. Do relay my best regards,
will you? Yes, it's been such a long time. You
were but a young child. I hardly recognized you
the other day. You've really filled out into a tall

young man. How tall are you?"

"Uh ... A metre eighty-four, I think."

"That's a good size. There, I think I know
what kind of first encounter you need. You're
about to have a very interesting and unexpected
encounter, and that's putting it mildly. I have
a friend called Tiresias. You'll see why when
you meet him. I don't actually know his real
name. Truth to say, I think nobody knows it.
He doesn't want anyone to know. He's quite
a character. Employed in a very elegant piano
bar at night. In the daytime, he begs on the
street. He says it teaches him to be humble.
An eccentric sort of fellow. You'll find him
tomorrow morning in the vicinity of the Pont
Mirabeau. He's on the bridge itself most of the
time. I'm going to call him at the bar to tell him
that you're coming. Just a moment, please."

I make the most of Cocteau's absence to
observe the gems strewn across the room. The
walls are lined with drawings and paintings,
the floor cluttered with all manner of objects:
paper, tea spoons, pens, handkerchiefs, a little
sculptured hand ... On impulse, I pick up the
ivory miniature and place it in the middle of my
own. It looks like the hand of a foetus. Sensing
Cocteau's return, I thrust it instinctively into
my pocket. This sleight of hand throws me once
again into a state of agitation, making it difficult
to keep my composure in front of Cocteau's
piercing eyes.

"He said he'd be delighted to make your acquaintance. He'll be expecting you tomorrow. You can go there when you wish, but let me give you a word of advice: don't put it off too long. He doesn't like to be kept waiting. I imagine you're in a hurry to shed your old skin, am I right? I see you're standing, ready to leave. Do you have to go already? Will you not have a cup of tea? It was sent to me directly from the Indies."

"It's just that my mother is expecting me..."

"Ah, mothers! I have one myself. I won't keep you any longer."

He places a long white hand on my shoulder, sliding down towards my chest. The over-intimate sensation puts a knot in my vocal chords.

"I'm looking forward to hearing from you, young man. Don't keep me waiting. I can't wait to bring out the butterfly slumbering under your clothes ..."

"J—"

"See you soon, my friend. Let me accompany you to the door."

"Goodbye ..."

"Goodbye, my dear. Call me. You can also reach me at my mother's, rue d'Anjou. Just across the square. The phone number is Anjou 31 16."

I float down the stairs without even feeling the steps under my feet, drifting on water. It feels like my throat is lined with a thick layer of fur. My hands keep the copyright imprint of the author's own fingers. Those long fingers that have held onto me, the way you clutch the hand of a man who has fallen into the water.

Outside, only a few scattered flakes flutter through the air. A white crumb comes to rest on my upraised forehead, melting on impact. The night is suddenly sweet. I can already feel the wings beating in my stomach. I've just become Angel Cocteau's protégé. Come to think of it, Angel is almost an anagram for Jean.

I begin to walk in the snow, kicking up the white powder into the lunar light of the gaslights. Life is lovely. I feel like walking all night. When I pass in front of my house, I'm in no condition to go to bed.

The little ivory hand in the pocket of my pants pushes against mine. I'm ashamed of having taken it and a bit scared he'll notice, but I'm so utterly happy that nothing can assail me. Cocteau's hand is there in my pocket, protecting me. I clench it tightly in my fist.

The Beggar

VIII

Alas, my sickening shyness stages a comeback the very next morning, squeezing me in its suffocating grip. I wake up feeling like a rat caught in the vice grip of a voracious maw. Its gastric juices are already spattering my face. I get a glimpse of the darkness of the tube leading down to my stomach.

"None of that! I shout." I give myself a big slap on the cheek. "You're going to go and see that Tiresias person this very morning!"

I get ready to leave and head off in the direction of Pont Mirabeau. When I get to the bridge, I find no-one who answers to the description of Tiresias. I inquire of a beggar but he doesn't seem to understand my question. He holds his open hand out in answer.

I search the surrounding area, crossing the bridge several times but there's no trace of anyone who might be Tiresias. I start to curse Cocteau, beginning to wonder as I grumble if he hasn't just been making fun of me all along.

I decide to wait on the bridge. After a whole

hour of shivering, I sink down onto the snow piled against the shoulder of the road. At long last, at the very moment I begin to think that the whole thing is a complete waste of time, I spot a shaggy-looking, thick-bearded bloke coming towards me.

Sauntering, he comes, printing holes in the snow as he advances towards me.

The man in question has no hat on his abundant head of hair. Despite the character's poise, there's a strange aura about him, something unsettling.

I notice when he stops in front of me that that uncanny feeling derives mostly from the fact that his right eye is missing. His eyeball isn't in its appointed place in the hollow of its orbit, giving his face a semi-absent, slightly inhuman air.

The skin hanging off the edges of his wound is sewn up any old how, as if the stitches have been put there in a hurry, in a botched, hit-and-miss with the needle sort of way.

Instead of the eye, there's a sort of bloated, chewed up half of an eyelid. Strictly speaking, it looks less like an eyelid than a piece of meat beaten thin and stuffed. Staring at him straight in the face makes me feel a little queasy.

This being said, the beard this man is wearing is decidedly surprising. It's a beard Karl Marx would have envied when his own beard was at the peak of its blossom.

The lower half of this ravaged face is a wilderness of luxuriating undergrowth. A bearded epiphany. A hairy proliferation. A beard that is more than thick. So arborescent you can picture buds growing out of it in the spring. I can hardly dare to imagine how much a lathering of shampoo under a nice warm shower would plump up this appendage. What hairy feast would then emerge from the tub.

The hair foam has crept over a good part of his face, ranging over his cheekbones. From the top of his shirt, a capillary froth spills out of his uncovered chest, as if the beard has taken root there to continue growing over the expanse of his pectorals. There is easily enough hair spread out over the top of this body to stuff a pillow.

Homo hairus is contemplating me with his remaining eye. He taps the ground in front of my feet with the tip of his cane. The bemused look on my face seems to displease him:

"Sir, you are sitting in my place."

"There aren't any pl-places here, that I kn-know of."

"I said you're sitting in my place."

Reluctantly, I get to my feet, muttering under my breath while my interlocutor sits down further on, a few paces away from the spot where I was sitting.

"I thought you said this was your place, and then you go and sit somewhere else ..."

"You shouldn't have got up, my lad. Rule

number one: never yield to a cad."

"You're making fun of me."

"Not at all, it was indeed my place. This is my bridge."

"You're saying this bridge belongs to you?"

"This is where I carry out my duties."

"So you're Tiresias?"

"That's more like it, my dear Oedipus. You are no doubt the young Thomas Hearse. Do put yourself at ease. Monsieur Jean has spoken very highly of you. I have the feeling I know you already. Come, sit beside me. We'll be more comfortably seated for conversation. Let me take you under my wing. Come on, don't stand there gawking."

"So you are Tiresias."

"Absolutely, my boy. Come closer, I can't see you properly. You will have noticed that I only have one eye. I have trouble seeing things in relief. So, I hear you want to be treated for excessive timidity. Tell me, are you deeply affected by this form of neurosis?"

"N-no, I-I ..."

"Alright, deeply affected. You're a virgin, if I'm not mistaken. Let me guess. The thought of accosting a young lady makes your legs tremble, it leaves you speechless and your lips start to quiver. You feel invisible most of the time and when someone looks at you, you find yourself unbearably plain. I have to say you're not particularly handsome. It's a good thing you're young.

At the age of nineteen, ugliness still looks
bearable. Well, you're fine, really. You aren't
disfigured. In any case, you'll have to cast a cold
eye on your physical appearance. Don't forget
you can still charm without being handsome.
It's all in the way you go about it. I manage to
do it with only one eye, so you … Don't worry,
I know exactly what you need. You did well
to go to Monsieur Jean. You're in luck. You've
caught his attention. But be careful. Don't fall
into the most obvious trap. I can see that your
admiration could easily change into love like
a bolt from the blue. A word of advice. Don't
fall for Cocteau. You don't yet possess what it
takes to weather the storm. You're not exactly
gorgeous and Cocteau likes young men who
look like Adonis. If you happen to be a budding
writer of genius, you may stand a chance, but
if you're just an aspiring scribbler, abstain. You
won't be able to keep him spellbound for very
long."

"I don't know what you're talking about. I'm
not an invert! Allow me to find what you say
rather improper. How d-dare you insinuate!"

"Ha! I see you are quite far from ready! You
know, Hearse, men, women, we're all more or
less the same. You may be a gentleman, and that
remains to be seen by the way, but you aren't
exactly enlightened. I mean, this is the 1930s!
I'm sure you're well aware that Monsieur Jean
has a fondness for young men and that he has

taken an interest in you not purely for pater-
nalistic and philanthropic reasons. He will no
doubt desire to have carnal knowledge of you
sooner or later. You can count on that. It's up
to you, to see if the game is worth the money. I
see I have shocked you. I'm speaking coarsely
without beating about the bush to see what you
can stomach. Anyway, all in good time. Let's
not rush. Let us start with something simple.
For your first exercise, we'll begin with a little
warm-up. The principle will be the same for
most of these tests: you'll have to set your habits
aside to get into the mind of someone you are
not. The mind of someone who is the polar
opposite to who you are at the moment. Or
who you think you are. To begin with, you will
therefore handle the pan by my side.

"But what if someone recognizes me! I'll lose
face. And my mother doesn't—"

"Your mother has nothing to do with this.
You aren't her property. You've reached the
age of consent even if you aren't twenty-one
yet. What you do is strictly your own business.
You're lucky enough to be unattached. Make
the most of it. Here, look, someone is coming
our way. Stick out the hat, like this. Learn to
welcome the coin ... My goodness, no. You're
as stiff as a scarecrow. You have to bend over
a little, adopt a hangdog expression, without
overdoing it in the process. Tell yourself you're
an outcast, that you've lost everything you ever

had. You're nothing, you're just a rat in a sewer, a big turd lying there in front of the boot of the passer-by. Whatever you do in life, the main thing is to be confident. If you're impersonating a cockroach, do it with conviction. Look at me. Imitate ... There, that's better. I'm going to leave now, I'll observe you from a distance."

"Don't leave! I mean ... I'll never be able to do this alone. What if someone recognizes me?"

"No one will recognize you. I can guarantee that. People avoid looking at tramps too closely. Off you go. Whatever you do, don't forget that you must try to establish eye contact with those who pass in front of you, even if they look reluctant. The aim of the first part of this test is also to keep your eyes up. It's crucial to maintain eye contact, regardless of whether the passer-by makes a disdainful face that expresses pity, disgust, incomprehension or indifference. Your aim for today will be to remain calm and collected. You should remain unaffected by feeling. You will have to avoid experiencing anxiety, joy, pain or pride of any kind. Tell yourself that you're a kind of black hole in which the expressions of those who pass are engulfed. Don't let their disdain sink into you, don't reject it either. You are a bank of fog in which everything fades to nothing. When you have mastered this technique, your phobia will for the most part be vanquished. So, I'll be watching your progress. See you later."

He gives me a kind of wink with his
sewn-up socket. His eyelid looks like a little
mouth mutely moving its lips.

I feel wretched, expatriated, expelled from
my cosy existence. Floundering in a wave of
melancholia, I wonder what the hell I'm doing
here. A pressing need to recover the chains of
my shyness sweeps over me again just as I see
another pedestrian passing on the other end of
the bridge.

He's coming my way.

I'm terribly ashamed. It feels like I'm back
in primary school, compelled by an untimely
bout of diarrhoea to drop my underpants in the
middle of a test in front of a crowd of classmates, cut to the quick by their laughter.

Here he comes.

I stare him straight in the eye. Remember
to keep looking him in the eye, no matter what
happens.

I realize I have the bearing of a robin
redbreast. I try with great difficulty to squeeze
the lemon that has just materialized at the back
of my mouth to extract an acidic hello.

The bastard passes, looking me up and down
with a mixed expression of disgust and surprise.
You can more or less decipher the following
thought in his eyes: *I didn't know that cockroaches
could reach that level of gluttony.*

And I'm not supposed to worry about what
other people think ...

Here's another pedestrian. It couldn't be worse this time round. An elegant young woman. Actually, there is worse, after all: to top it all, she's beautiful, even startlingly so. Slit skirt, fruity smile. My eyes are beginning to water. I hope she isn't also generous and compassionate.

Of course she is.

She's heading right for me, her hand in her bag.

This time, it's not a lemon I have in my throat, it's a whole watermelon. My voice is nothing but a tiny pip, a mosquito smothered in a huge tub of honey.

I start nodding mechanically.

"Hllo, Miz. Thunks, Mzz."

A slight tremor shoots through the woman's silky frame as she bends over in front of me to deposit the coin into the limpness of my hat. She shoots me a brief, searching glance. The elegant outline of her fingers stands out from her hip. The index finger of her hand remains delicately curved up after setting down the coin, as if it's pointing in the direction of paradise. A faint stain of blue ink on that finger. The veil over her eyes. Her almost shy eyelid. A shade of touching awkwardness in the way she moves. I will probably never see her again. I swallow a large chunk of watermelon.

The next pedestrians are decidedly less unsettling so I manage to spit a mouthful

of watermelon at each greeting. All kinds of
people file past: the young, contemptuous social
climber (the high-ranking official type whose
personality is reduced to the handkerchief
sticking out so becomingly from the pocket of
his blazer); bald, greasy forty-year-old (trumpet-
shaped nose with one muted nostril); hobbling
old lady; grandson in his twenties at her side,
dressed from top to toe in his black Sunday
best and old before his time; street urchins
distractedly licking the seepage from their
nostrils; little girls with upraised eyebrows and
sidelong stares, little red pouting mouths.

Each has his own way of dropping the coin
in the hat. After a few hours, I start to distin-
guish a range of different types. There's the coin
laid down respectfully, ceremoniously, the way
you deposit a little pebble on the gravestones in
Jewish cemeteries; there's the coin that's flicked
your way, from afar, eyes turned away, as if
disposing of evidence.

I'm occasionally the recipient of coins left
reluctantly, the kind of coin you put down
hesitantly and come back to fetch fifteen
minutes later.

Of all coins, the one I hate the most, the coin
held with the tip of the fingers like a snotty
handkerchief dropped in a spittoon. The kind of
coin that means here you are, young free-loader,
you don't deserve that.

The one you prefer of course: the golden

crest, deposited like an offering on a velvet-covered cushion, with a sweet smile that stays imprinted on your retina. A coin that's round as a mouth. You feel like putting your lips up against it.

IX

"All these impressions really show the extent
to which you find it difficult to clear your mind
and rid yourself of all value judgments, all
response, all seductive or resentful interaction",
Tiresias faults me, on returning. He twiddles
with his beard, pulling it out like a spring.

"I couldn't agree more, but it's so hard!
What you're asking me to do is the equivalent
of negating human interaction. I'll end up being
autistic, instead of just sh-shy!"

"Your problem resides exactly in your
excessive receptivity. You feel things too
deeply. You go into such detail. Which is good
for writing, but not for life. You also excuse
yourself for being there. You step aside as soon
as anyone tries to take your place. When all's
said and done, how would you define shyness?"

"It's ..."

"Above all, it's a lack of belief in yourself.
I want to teach you that self-confidence can
be achieved without needing to trust others.
People spend their time placing their confidence

in individuals who can stab them in the back, when a total stranger can save your life and lose his own. What you say about your voice is highly revealing. We'll work on your vocal cords later on. If everything goes well and you don't succumb to the dangers of these trials, you'll have enough self-confidence to seduce and pick your nose at the same time. In the meantime, you're going to pursue today's experiment for a few days, until you're comfortable with the role."

"I'll never be able to play the role convincingly dressed like this. These leather ankle boots are brand new. I'm wearing a herring-bone suit made of English tweed. The reason I got so few coins after nine hours of begging is simply that I'm too well dressed, too young, too healthy looking for the part. Most people probably think I'm a repulsive idler, a shame to modern society."

I'm under the impression I've spotted a sort of insect floundering about in the curlicues of his beard. It even looks like they're teeming in there. I have a mounting desire to go and grub about in that undergrowth to extract the intruder.

"Don't forget that the Wall Street Crash ruined a great number of well-off families and that the ranks of our aristocracy are full of rich people who have fallen on hard times. The bourgeoisie is completely impoverished.

Think of your clothes and your youth as but an additional obstacle to overcome. The more people will glare at you, the more you will be able to work on your state of serenity."

With his swordstick, he starts to scrape off a layer of ice stuck to the pavement before continuing his speech.

"One more thing. I have the feeling that you are confusing this state of grace I've mentioned with indifference. Your goal shouldn't be to cut yourself off entirely from the world; you should aim to be satisfied with everything. Perceive everything that happens to you—good or bad—as a means of improving yourself. Each event, no matter how small, should become a branch or a twig in the tree of your personality. Don't let it get to you. I can sense that you're a promising pupil. Monsieur Jean is in agreement with me on this. He has asked me about you and is much in sympathy with your family, given what happened to your father. Which is why we've decided to collaborate in the furthering of your education. Monsieur Jean will be in charge of your night life; I will be your mentor in the daytime. Of course, we shall retain the right to reverse this principle from time to time, if the need arises."

"It's very kind of you, but I'm not a pupil anymore. I must attempt to find real employment now. My mother is relentless in her wish to have me work, as the benefits she receives thanks to her widow's allowance are insufficient to support our needs."

Tiresias's lips suggest a flicker of a smile under his beard. I can no longer see the insect. It must have burrowed down somewhere into the labyrinth of his beard.

"What's your aim in life?"

"I've always wanted to be a no-novelist. In fact, I'd like to write like Cock-cock-Cocteau … I would have liked to have written The Holy Terrors, but that's already been done. I've no idea if I have any real talent."

"Well, in order to write, you have to live a little first, don't you? To write a novel, you have to view the world from an unfamiliar vantage point. The easiest path when you're an absolute beginner is to perceive life either from below or from above. If you describe people the way an office clerk would, socially integrated and encrusted on his chair, you're going to bore everyone, yourself included."

To my surprise, Tiresias crouches down to confect a small snowball. He starts to shove it roughly into the lip-like cavity left in the hollow of his missing eye. The effect is both grotesque and mesmerizing. His face looks like a fluffy egg laid in a nest of twigs. He stares out at me through the eyelash-framed snowy monocle, putting on a gentlemanly voice:

"What you would need is to get a position under the pen-pusher's desk so you get an idea of how to describe what's happening under the table, to get a closer look at the stains on the soles of the desk clerk's shoes to get a hint of the places he goes to, to get a whiff of the primitive's hairy legs, stick an eye into the tunnel of the scribbler's trousers and use it as a telescope to discover the world. Being a writer means being able to make everything interesting, even boredom itself. It means being able to savour every detail, no matter how trivial. There's no fruitless experience or irredeemable ugliness for the author. A true writer knows how to transform even suffering and tragedy. We may not succeed in making you into a writer, but if we manage to make you think like one, you'll be able to withstand any test without being destroyed by it. This being said, if you find life from below too pitiful", he adds, expelling the snow eye from its socket with a forward thrust of his head, "you can also adopt the perspective of the angel who flies above everything. I would personally opt for the lower angle. I find it more interesting, more accessible, especially for a beginner: everything will seem larger than life, closer. More tangible. If I had to choose between immanence and transcendence, I would go for the first, to begin with. It's up to you. You can always sample both in turn. In the meantime, let me offer you this job. You'll be my employee, an attendant on Mirabeau Bridge. In exchange for the money you earn in this way, I will provide

you with a single meal a day which you will
savour with a keen appetite. At the end of the
day, you'll report back to me and when the
evening comes you'll pass into Monsieur Jean's
care. He will tell you in advance where you
are to find him. He'll show you the earth seen
from above, the lives of angels, flights of love,
the omniscient outlook, all that. If you want to
stand a chance of becoming a writer, you'll have
to experience our crucible."

"But what will I tell my mother when she
asks me to account for my time?"

"Tell her simply that you have found
employment in Switzerland, say, or that you
have to travel."

"What if she comes across me one day
sitting on the bridge?"

"She won't come this way. People always go
through the same places and if what Monsieur
Jean says is anything to go by, you don't live
anywhere close. Paris isn't exactly a village.
Anyway, the sun is setting. Cocteau awaits.
He'll meet you at the Montparnasse cemetery.
You must go there without further delay. See
you tomorrow morning, then. I'll be watching
you from afar, the way I did today. Be there at
eight, on the dot."

Before I can ask for further information, the
large, sombre mass of Tiresias's figure is already
mingling with the colours of the dusk. I rise
from the white earth fallen from the sky.

X

Montparnasse cemetery, at last.

A strange meeting place.

I feel like Huckleberry Finn. When I reach
the gates of the graveyard, they're locked of
course, which forces me to scale the colossal
perimeter wall. An experience which leaves
me with a long bleeding gash on my calf and
a trickle of sweat that sticks to my clothes like
strawberry jam.

Darkness starts to spread over the gravestones. There's no one to be seen. He could have
given me some indication about which part of
the cemetery he means to meet me. The place
seems so utterly empty. I wend between the
tombstones, as if I'm finding my way through
the vast granite beds of a boarding school
dormitory.

I'm suddenly scared my nocturnal mentor
has hidden himself in a vault to give me a
terrifying educational surprise in the middle of
a deserted cemetery. I'm afraid to see him leap
out from behind every grave.

Not having been able to locate the meeting place, I head for the grave in which my great-great-grandfather on my father's side lies buried for over half a century. I go and visit his grave from time to time to tend it and to savour the mellifluous inscription it bears:

EMILE HONEY AND HIS SPOUSE MADELEINE

I picture them in Arcadia, glued to each other, sampling honey at every meal, lying down in a bed of treacle, sucking a corner of pillow until they awaken. When morning comes, you pour a little honey on the bicycle chain to go and work in the fields. At work, you harvest the honey on the ground, raking in the bees fallen from the honey trees in bloom, gathering them in a large bronze-coloured sack, to shell them with Madeleine. Pop! You uncork the head of a little bee to make its honey capsule flow into the jar. A couple like none other, confected out of gold and ambrosia.

Behind me, I hear a voice call out:

"Thomas Hearse? Angel Heurtebise would like to bestow a kiss on you. The blue lips of the skies deposit their colour on your cheek."

"Monsieur Cocteau?"

"Eau de cock?! Cock of fire, you mean! I am the fiery bird that wakes at the infernal dawn."

"I can't see you! Where are you?"

"I am life seen from above."

"Are you in a tree?"

"Tree? What tree are you talking about? Everything around me is a fiery bush! My hair is on fire, my lashes are stars, my eyes are a bonfire. Find all hope, ye who enter here."

I finally catch sight of Cocteau perched on a yew tree, his head leaning against a bow still covered in snow.

"Be careful, Sir, you might fall."

"Fall? These wings I unfold are not bound with mere church candlewax. They have been tempered in the sun."

"Mr Cocteau, do you wish to come down onto my back?"

"Like the unshakeable old man on Sinbad's shoulders. I will climb down on top of you. Move as close as you can to the branch. Closer. Hold still. Place your shoulder against the trunk, will you? There were are … I'm on. Cross the stream, now, so I may feel myself walking on the waves, straddling my aquatic steed. We will be a two-headed man. Surely you agree that two heads are better than one? Keep going, we must get back on dry land. Giddy-up! Giddy-up! Fare onwards, my steed!"

"Have you been drinking, Monsieur Cocteau?"

"Drinking? Drinking involves a liquid, a basely tangible substance! Know that I do not consume the fruits of the earth. I breathe

only clouds, and nourish myself with celestial
fumes. Opium, my dear friend, is a telescope
for the spiritually near-sighted. It's the smoke
that signals to man the presence of the gods.
By golly, you are a solid steed. I would have
thought you frailer. Faster, horse! The current is
pulling us towards the rocks."

I thought he too would be slighter. Jean
Cocteau weighs a ton and a half. To make
matters worse, he starts to jump up and down
on my shoulders like a crazed child. Stoically
clenching my teeth, I tighten my hold on Jean
Cocteau's heels while he frolics in the air.

Twice in a row, his right shoe gives me
a kick in the back. Only because this is Jean
Cocteau do I comply without balking. It feels
like Balzac or Corneille is straddling my
shoulders.

But now Jean Cocteau's lace comes undone
in mid jolt. Jesus Christ's shoe slips from my
hand and we trip over a bed of roses. I fall face
forward onto a rose and Jesus plants his eagle's
beak in the earth. We burst out laughing at the
sight of his shoe that has landed on the slab of a
tombstone.

"I have tasted the soil and you have tasted
my blood! Come, you have a crown of thorns
on your cheek, my little one. Let me remove it
... there ... there ... and ... there we are. All you
have left now are a few pearls of blood. I have a
handkerchief somewhere. Wait, don't move."

Gloved in a handkerchief that's white as the snow, Cocteau's long hand comes to rest on my cheek. With his other hand, he dabs at my nostril. And now he puts the handkerchief back in his pocket, grabs me by the ear and starts to caress my lobes gently, running his finger along the grooves of my auricular appendage. My ear is nothing but a receptacle of sensations.

"Come, let me pour some words into your ear. Come closer. Don't be shy."

I do his bidding despite myself. He comes closer. A panther in ambush. I feel the feline breath of the big white cat on my neck. I do my best not to move, awaiting his words with a terrifying intensity. What will he say to me? I await the voice of God.

I receive it like a wave of salt water.

Cocteau slips his tongue into my ear. I feel its panting warmth. It penetrates into the shell of my ear like a remorseless mollusc.

I break away abruptly, no longer knowing where I am, nor what is happening. I rush down a row of tombstones.

"Thomas! Wait. Don't leave! Come, don't be angry. This is but a trifle!"

I lean against the granite of a tombstone and put my head in my hands to try to think. I sense his steps coming closer behind me. The snow crumples and tears under his tread. It feels as if he has a hundred feet, that a giant centipede is staggering towards me.

And then a terrible thing happens.

I feel his long burning hands on my hips.
They slowly descend on my buttocks and start
to fondle my crotch. I tremble as if they are
branding me with a red-hot iron.

I clutch the stones. A hollow opens up inside
me and I feel a sudden unexpected anticipation
between my buttocks.

He slowly lowers my pants, pulling down
my underwear in one swift stroke. He settles me
over a tombstone on all fours. I crush the snow
on the stone, kneading it between my fingers.

Something wet comes into me like molten
iron poured into my cleft, jabbing, thrusting into
the place where I feel the intensity of longing.
It's like a stitch, but a delicious one, right in the
middle. A blade of hunger opens up between
my legs, a tunnel of pleasure wending its way
into my flesh. My penis nods in approval like a
stiffened dog's tail.

What happens then is out of the realm of
the possible. I find myself figuring in a surreal
painting.

Max Ernst, and then Salvador Dali, search
and lick my sphincter until the tears well up
in my eyes. Their prehensile tongues penetrate
deep between my buttock cheeks. Max is
kneading me. His long slug licks back and forth.
Dali spills his ants over my body and I watch
them crawling over my buttocks. He crushes
and kneads a mashed dough of ants over the

length of my back. He sticks and shoves hard and soft shapes inside me. They rush into the breaches of my mouths and dissolve each in turn.

XI

"You're late," he grouses.

"Yes, I … I'm sorry …"

"I won't hold it against you this time. But in future know that employees must be on time at their posts. Here, sit on the footpath, I've cleared the snow away. You seem a bit drowsy today. Did you not sleep well?"

"Yes, well, I haven't slept a wink."

"Monsieur Jean and I are both in favour of the strong-arm approach. Are you feeling any less timid?"

"Uh … I haven't thought about it yet. You know, I really haven't got a clue what's going on these days …"

"Your pants is terribly soiled. Where have you been? Those stains look like blood. Have you slept in a slaughterhouse?"

"I … I don't know anymore. I'm not even sure where I spent the night. I know I walked … along a river."

"Well, in any case, you look transformed! The rings under your eyes give your features

more character. They give your ugliness a
slightly tragic touch. A shade of beyond the
grave. I'll say, you seem almost dark! Anyway,
let's get back to work. I'd like you to write a
letter."

"A letter?"

"Yes, a letter. Address it to the tramp you
see over there."

"But what on earth am I going to write? I
don't know him from Adam."

"Take it as an exercise in style. Do you want
to become a writer, or not? Just write about
yourself. Tell him who you are, what you aspire
to. Describe your parents to him. You know, talk
to him about anything that strikes your fancy.
Here you are, a few sheets of paper and a pen.
Don't forget that if you want to hold on to this
post, you'll have to provide quality work. Have
a good day. See you this evening."

To have to write a letter, in the state I'm in.

I'll never be able to concentrate. Cocteau in
the cemetery ... How will I be able to get over
it? I feel like I've become someone else. I don't
know what I've turned into.

It's all so absurd. A letter to a tramp. Why
not a letter to the postman? This is getting too
strange for words. I feel like leaving. Finding a
cushy job in a nice, ordinary office with normal
people. Shyness is a comfort, after all. For
goodness sake, a letter to the vagabond! Letter
to my ear!

I have to say that I can't really relate to my own ear anymore either. All I have left on my head is a single ear with a living snail on the other side instead of a hearing instrument. I might well write a letter to my gastropod holes.

I've never felt anything like it. And yet I wish only to gaze upon women. As soon as they lower their eyes, I devour their bodies.

But at this very moment, I have an irrepressible urge to feel that tongue at my heels. A pack of tongues. My fiddle wagging in front of me like a tail. A fire in my loins. I have to hold Cocteau in my arms, no matter what the cost.

I was in love with his work. I'm now in love with the man. So, that's what being an invert is. An inversion of the usual order.

Inverted, I stop the flow of time in my head, I turn counter-clockwise.

Mirabeau Bridge, 2 February 1932

Dear Tramp,

Let me present myself. I am the tramp opposite you on the other side of the bridge. I'm not too sure what I've done to deserve this. I wanted to become a writer; I find myself a beggar. I've been led to believe that there's a hidden link between these two occupations. What are your thoughts on this?

*Whatever the case may be, I've applied myself
to plying this new trade because I'm ready to do
whatever it takes to become an author. If it means
becoming a beggar, prostituting myself, selling
my soul, I will do it.*

*Alas, I am prompted by a fervent need to put
things down on paper, without really knowing
what to write. It's exactly the same when I meet
other people. I don't know what to say to them.
Their faces appear to me as blank pages, impossible to fill.*

*I'm too young and have not experienced
the pleasure of having travelled far afield. My
childhood was neither happy nor miserable. Just
uneventful. I have nothing to say about it. A few
anecdotes, perhaps, but nothing substantial.*

*Like everyone else, I lived through the war,
which could in itself have offered a fruitful source
of stories and suffering to recount, but nothing
can come of it as I was too small to remember
anything at all. You might say that the Great
War slipped right through my fingers. I was born
in 1913. My little nose wasn't developed enough
to sniff out the Great War. While thousands
of people were living in utter despair, I was
savouring my wet nurse's breast.*

*My life is really of no interest whatsoever.
An average childhood, a dull time at school, few
or no friends, parents with no imagination. The
only remarkable feature of my existence was
my father's suicide. That's when you say: but*

that's a perfect episode for a novel! Well, you're
wrong. For there was no heartbreak or mystery
in that suicide. The reasons for his act were
limpid and predictable. He was bored with his
work (little office worker), his wife was more or
less frigid (I believe she conceived me out of a
sense of propriety). He was incapable of speaking
to his son; he had no hobby and didn't enjoy
conversation.

True, he committed suicide without leaving
a valedictory note, which might suggest a little
mystery, but in his case, the presence of a
handwritten letter would have constituted more
of a mystery than the absence of one. He never
experienced the need to put pen to paper and I
think he wouldn't have known what to write. And
so we transmitted nothingness to each other, from
father to son.

I cannot even complain about his absence,
as he was eternally present, always there in
the evenings, but in appearance at least always
empty. Even his hugs were hollow. He would
embrace the void, his arms in the shape of a zero.

You will retort: you see, it's a very fruitful
subject. But the story ends there. I don't feel
the need to say anything more about my father.
I feel nothing for him. I don't even think I love
him. He vanished completely two years ago, and
we're already used to his absence. My mother
never spoke of him again. After his death, she
bought herself a dog. My father didn't like

canine creatures and couldn't stand the thought
of having one at home. Is that why she went as
far as to give my father's name to the dog? The
notion was hateful to me at first, but I finally got
used to it.

As for my mother, she's almost as unfathomable as my father. They had that in common,
at least. I think I detect in her voice a measure of
satisfaction when she raises her acerbic, English-
sounding voice: "sit, Albert!" or "Lie down,
Albert!" or "Albert, do you want me to kick
you?!" She's always liked order. Our flat is so
tidy it looks like an ethnographic museum.

That's how things are. My brief story ends
there. I've finished my studies and I live with
my mother. We don't say much to each other. At
most, "can you hand me the salt", or "you should
find employment."

You could argue that my ugliness is an
advantage when it comes to becoming a poet, but
can ugliness really be used as a yardstick allowing
you to reach the heights of creativity?

Quasimodo does climb to the topmost part
of the bell tower to sound the greatness of his
soul, but I do not possess sufficient quantities of
ugliness. I am unfortunately far from possessing
Quasimodo's sublimely unprepossessing physical
traits.

Hideous ugliness could have inspired in me
a ferocious, creative hatred of both God and man.
But nothing has come of mine as I am not really

repulsive; just plain in a banal sort of way. My face doesn't elicit disgust, merely boredom. When you see me, you just think he has no charm at all, if you even manage to formulate a specific thought concerning me, as I hardly stimulate reflection. No one is tempted while observing me to pursue contemplation. I would even say that people experience a certain weariness in having to consider me carefully. When I have to explain myself at a counter to buy a train ticket, for instance, I notice that the clerk gets irritable, as if he had something more important to do with his time than sell tickets to the likes of me.

Perhaps that's why I try to write. To turn my trite plainness into a thing of beauty. But how to find a subject for a novel? As I've already said, my imagination is particularly lame. My only hope, my only springboard to success in reaching the heights of literature: the serendipitous fact that my father happened to meet Cocteau when I was still a child.

So that's the story of my life up to now. I meet Cocteau to become a writer and he entrusts me to a man who advises me to become a beggar. Here I am, apprenticed to a vagrant, in the first stage on the road to beggarliness. Will that allow me to find the impetus to write a novel?

Must one reach rock bottom to bounce back up, Brother Beggar, what do you think? Like you, I've now become a sort of lowly gargoyle, a bell fallen to the ground. I wonder about my vocation

*as a fallen bell. What does one feel when one
becomes a real tramp? Why does one become a
tramp in the first place? Could you enlighten me
on this point?*

*Is there a difference between a beggar and a
vagabond? I'd like to say that the beggar stays put
like a bell. You always find him in the same place.
On a bridge, on a bench, in front of a cathedral.
The beggar is a bell that chimes at every hour.
He's there from dawn to dusk, come rain or shine.
Despite himself, he imitates the office worker: he
arrives at his workplace at a given hour, settles
down on the same office desk pavement, sells hot
air and finds ways of selling more of it.*

*By contrast, the vagabond departs as much
as possible from the bureaucratic model, defying
all stability. He's a disappointed angel, but not a
fallen one. He turns his back on ordinary life and
chooses to tramp about, free as a nomad.*

*Anyway, enough speechifying. I realize I've
been long-winded for once. That may be a start,
who can tell? I don't know you, but I can see
from the way you stole a good part of my clientele
yesterday, that you are an old hand at this. At
a guess, I would say that you are one of those
anchored, unmovable beggars, riveted for life. Tell
me if I'm wrong. Were you there when Apollinaire
wrote his poem, when the Eiffel Tower was being
erected?*

*Yours sincerely,
Thomas Hearse*

XII

When I hand the letter to Tiresias he reads
it with a sullen expression on his face, grunting
gently from time to time, scratching his beard.

"It won't be enough to seduce Cocteau, but
it isn't bad for a start. I'm even tempted to give
it to the tramp in question. I wonder how he'll
take it. Let's see what he has to say."

"I take it you're joking."

"Not at all. You can tell by the look on my
face when I'm joking."

"Please tell me you're not going to hand my
letter to that drifter!"

"Why ever not? I'm curious to find out how
you get yourself out of a sticky situation."

"I'm warning you. If you do that, I'll leave
this place right now. And I won't come back!"

"It would be a mistake on your part. My aim
is to save you from yourself. You don't know it
yet, but I'm going to save your life."

"Oh, how grandiose. I need nobody to save
me. My life isn't actually in danger right now.
But I will be in danger of dying of shame if you

give him that letter."

"If you say so ..."

"Hand me the letter!"

"I'm afraid I can't give it back to you."

"Fine, keep it then but please don't hand it on to that wretch. Imagine what it's like to be in his shoes. There's no knowing how he might react."

"I see we're going to have to awaken your taste for the unexpected ... Bear this in mind: wisdom means being mad when circumstances call for it."

Upon which, without saying another word, he departs. I watch him leave, steeped in my usual stupefaction whenever it comes to Tiresias's shenanigans.

Suddenly, although he is walking on the opposite footpath, I see him cross the road and veer towards the tramp. Before I can get up and cry out, he bends over in front of the vagabond to hand him my letter.

I'm about to get up and disappear when I see Tiresias pointing straight at me.

Tiresias beats a hasty retreat, his mission accomplished. I watch the tramp rise to his feet and head straight for me.

Paralyzed by my own stupor, pinned like a butterfly against the parapet, my eyes rolling, I face the man hobbling towards me.

He seems stocky now and threatening.

He comes to a stop before me, takes out a handkerchief as large as a pillowcase, filthy as the

floor of a slaughterhouse and blows his nose like
a trumpet, puffing like a sperm whale returning
to the surface.

The stubby fingers he lays on my shoulder
are black with grime. The stink that emanates
from his rags reminds me of a sick rodent. The
acrid scent sticks in my throat, drilling into my
nostrils like a chemical substance violently effer-
vescing. A stray dog must have relieved itself on
his clothes.

His healthiest teeth are yellow. His rheumy
eyes bulge. His forehead is so furrowed—made
puffy by his wrinkles and the fatty foods he
ingests—that his skin is pleated in greasy bulges
topped with lumps of flesh. There are what
I can only call croutons of dirt in the soup of
his beard. His shaggy hair is stamped with the
shape of the pillow. It's standing straight up
like a clump of trees, like a hairy version of
Wuthering Heights.

His head nodding ascent, the ragged wretch
addresses me with his gruff rasping voice. The
sound that issues from his lips is more like a
gargle than anything else. What he has just said
sounds vaguely like "ghaurrôrrr". You can hear
the spelling mistakes when he speaks.

I answer his gargle with my own stammering
word:

" ... H-helloo ..."

" ... "

" ... "

"Arrorr ... I hhave as you might say ... a thing ... ta ask ya".

"... gyeah ..."

"As you might say ... a favour ... by mutual agreement."

"Yes ..."

"Dere's a man who's just given me a sorta dispatch. I can't understand whas written dere. Ken ya explain dis paper? He tol me ta ask ya."

The breath he exhales onto my face is as fetid as an infected crocodile's. I have trouble deciding whether his tone is aggressive or if he's just too much of a wino to be gentle.

"Wh-why?"

The pudgy man's face takes on a cunning expression. He sticks his little finger in his ear, searching for something complex to retrieve.

"What do ya tink, little fella?"

Slotted into the right place, his baby finger starts to wriggle about in a frenzy deep inside his ear.

"I-I don't know."

"Dya know de man who wrote de letter?"

"... Not that much."

He pulls his little finger out of his ear, inspects the unctuous matter he has been able to extract and is careful to spread it discreetly onto his rags.

"Strange sort of fella, isn't he? Not very natural, that eye of his ... Slightly disgusting, don't you think? ... And dat beard ... looks like the nest of an albatross. I've never seen a tuft the size of dat. Anyway, as dey say, to each his own disgusts ... He told me you could read whas written on dis letter here. Apparently, tsfor me."

"Oh, really?" I say. My jaw starts to tremble.

"You have to read it to me ... by mutual agreement."

" ... "

"Are ya constipated?"

"Uh ... ne-no ..."

"Could ya not speak a bit louder? My ears are all clogged up."

"I said no!"

"No need to get gressive! I'd just like ya to read me da letter. Can understand not everyone's been to school. I can't read, dya know what I'm saying?! I'd a liked to habeen a Frence teacher. But that wasn't possible. My father he didn't want me ta do me studies, like."

" ... "

"Dya understand, or doancha?"

"Yes, yes, of course ..."

"Dya know howta read at least?"

"Yes ... I mean ... not ... not that well."

"Right, let's just say that ya can. Go on den, here, take it, I'm all ears ... by mutual agreement, like."

Why did I not have the presence of mind to say that I didn't know how to read either! I'm now faced with my own inane letter. I tell

myself I have to improvise. Tell him whatever
comes into my head. But my mind is a blank.
I'm about to say "Dear Tramp" when I catch
myself and utter the following in an ill-assured
voice:

"Dear ... Sir ..."

"Dear Sir. I like dat. Dear Sir ..."

The hobo starts scratching his buttock, as if
to put up a bold front.

"Dear Sir ..."

"Again?"

"No, it's ... I have trouble deciphering the
handwriting ..."

"Tell me something. Can you tell me who
wrote dis?"

"This letter? Uh ... there's a name. It's ... It
says ... Tiresias. That's it. Tiresisas."

"Who's dat?"

"It's the gentleman who gave you the letter."

"Really? He coulda told me...
Whatelsedoeseesay?"

The hobo starts to dig deeper into the ragged
depths of his pants as if he's trying to drill a
hole in there.

"He says that ... he'd like ... to be a writer."

"Whyze tellin me dat?"

"Uh ... I've no idea. You know, I don't know
him that well."

"An hows he goanta become a writer?"

"He says ... he wants to meet a writer to
turn into one himself."

"By magic, like."

"Yes, that's it, by magic. He knows a ... a woman who publishes novels. And he wants her to ... to make love to him ... so he can be a writer."

"Seems difficult ta me."

"No, he says he knows he can be ... in some way ... fertilized."

"Fertilized? Told ya. The guy's unnatural. Would he by any chance be as you might say an invert?"

" ... It's possible. He adds that the really important thing for him is to become a writer. He says he's neither man nor woman, ultimately, but a writer."

The tramp arches his back to get a deep scratch of his bottom.

"I taught he wasn't a writer yet. Aren't these learned people a bit soft in de head?"

"He says he wants to possess the writer. He wants to suck his writer's blood. To squeeze his throat like a lemon to gather the words that trickle out of his lips. He wants to rip the writing out of his belly. To rummage through his carcass to find the place where the best words are hidden. To penetrate him. Rip out his heart, the way a warrior sodomizes another vanquished warrior in the thick of the battle to lay hold of his powers ..."

"... Jesus ... are ya sure we're talkin about de fella who walked over back there? He looked a bit odd alright, but gentle, not gressive ..."

"Absolutely. Look, it says so right here. See. Ti-re-sias."

"What I doan understand is why he wants to write all this ... to me."

"He says he would like to get to know you more intimately."

"Intimately? Virgin whore! He's a total invert! Here, give me dat letter so I can tear it to shreds. Filty writer. I'm off ta beg fer alms on anudder bridge. Can't be left in peace without a dirty stinkin writer to come and stick der disgustin ideas in yer head. You'd be wise ta leave too. You look a bit infected already. Come, I'll show ya a bridge where you'll be left in peace ... Come, come on, I tell ya! By de way, my name's Louis de Wreck ... It's a pleasure ta meet ya. Go on, shake my hand."

As soon as Louis lies down for the night three bridges down the road, in the miasma of his blankets—after holding forth for two hours—I give him the slip and make my way back to Mirabeau Bridge. My rage against Tiresias has abated and all I aspire to now is to breathe normally again, far from Louis' heady effluvia, and find out what's in store for me next. I finally catch a glimpse of the verdigris-coloured bridge with its two outcropping bronze giants and their tapering trumpets. Tourists are still scampering like lemmings towards the Eiffel lighthouse.

When I reach the bridge, someone is sitting
on the snow in my place. I have the uncanny
impression that that person is me, and that I'm
approaching myself: the position the person has
adopted is exactly the same as the one I usually
take. One leg stretched out, the other tucked in,
my chin raised. It can only be Tiresias.

"I do a fair imitation of you, don't you think?"

"Mr Cocteau."

"Mr Hearse."

"Good evening ... Are you not afraid of
being recognized. I mean, your reputation."

"Oh, I'll never be famous enough for
biographers to write later on that on the
second of February 1932 at eight o'clock in the
evening, Jean Cocteau sat down like a tramp
on Mirabeau bridge—the renowned bridge
on which, a few decades earlier, Apollinaire
himself wrote a poem as he was doing a wee in
the Seine. You know the poem? Under Mirabeau
runs the sanies ... You know, it's good to take
leave of yourself from time to time. It's so
restful to forget that I'm Jean Cocteau. And I
just love to impersonate people. I used to do a
really good imitation of Proust in the old days.
I'll show you my imitation of Breton and Eluard
when the occasion arises—my friends find them
rather droll. Just a moment ago, I was trying to
get an idea of who you were by reproducing
your gestures. I observed you this morning
with Tiresias. You're very sensitive, as much

an introvert as I am an extrovert. But judging
from what Tiresias tells me, you're self-ef-
facing only on the inside. You can apparently
be quite caustic at times. Which is something
I like. That's exactly it: you're a butterfly still
imprisoned in its caterpillar. I fear that in your
case time alone will not suffice to open the
butterfly's cage. If we aren't a bit rough with
you, you could remain in a larval state your
whole life. I hope I didn't go too far the other
night ..."

"... It was ..."

"I felt the butterfly rustle within you. I
licked its wings a little—so to speak. Come
and sit by my side. We can savour the evening
together. Come, I won't bite you, not this time,
at least. You know, the other night, I may have
had too much pipe. I must have smoked more
than ten in the afternoon. If I don't cut down,
I may have to go into rehab for drug addiction
and suffer all the horrors that ensue. Mind
you, I'm often at my most prolific at the clinic.
There's nothing to do there, the walls are white,
the nurses too. You discover an irresistible urge
to fill the blankness and you start to write. The
last time, I penned *Opium*, which immediately
prompted me to give birth to *The Holy Terrors*.
They came out of me like ink twins, two
monsters, pure as the blankness of oblivion.
Tiresias tells me you're particularly taken with
this work. It's true, a lot of young people like

that book. I'm not too sure why, exactly. Is it thanks to Paul's love of Dargelos or Elizabeth's for Paul? Incest of homosexuality? What do you think, my dear Thomas? You haven't said a word."

"I … maybe it's just forbidden fruit … Young people like things to be forbidden. And impossible love … that's always attractive. And it's got so many beautiful images. Maybe that's it. The first snowball that enters Paul's mouth is an incredible symbol … It's the Eucharist, death, innocence, penetration, violence, and the magic of snow, all rolled into one … I know that passage by heart, and many others as well."

"Well, I'm delighted to hear this! I feel your butterfly flapping in its chrysalis, my friend! I wonder if you aren't already well groomed for a literary salon. This being said, I think we should start with a coffee house, if you don't mind. My friends and I prefer to meet in cafés. It so happens that Max has asked me if I was coming out to the Splendid this evening."

"Max …?"

"Don't pull that face. It makes you look like a spaniel. You've nothing to fear. He's as kind as can be and not that Breton for a Breton. You'll see, he's very open-minded. I'm talking about Max Jacob. You've heard of him, I trust? He's the greatest Breton poet of all time."

"Oh, Max Jacob. Yes, I've read a few of his poems."

"So, what do you think, shall we go?"

"Well ..."

"Oh, come on, don't make a fuss. Get up on my shoulders, dear Butterfly. Come, come! Get up on the rail. It's my turn now. There we go ... Do be careful not to fall. That's it ... Phew! You're heavy. Good Lord! How much do you weigh? Let us go. I'm going to call you Mr. Butterfly, it's less macabre. I have to say your surname is a little heavy-going."

I cross part of Paris on Jean Cocteau's shoulders. He does his best to carry me to our destination despite a growing pain in the neck.

The evening unfolds in a haze of opium smoke, cigarettes and various kinds of alcohol. Which doesn't stop me from feeling terrified to the end of the evening when I find out that around the table at the Splendid Café are not only Max Ernst and Max Jacob, but also André Gide, Colette and Pablo Picasso (who doesn't deign to look at me all evening).

Mr Picasso is a mine of information and anecdotes. He tells us that when he buys something expensive he doodles a signed drawing on the back of his cheques to make sure people don't cash them. Everyone is full of admiration, especially Cocteau who's looking at him as if he's Buddha's latest reincarnation (it's true they're both as stubby as each other).

After first enthusiastically presenting me as "Mr Butterfly, one of my protégés", Cocteau forgets me on the spot. I feel without substance, a sort of phantom seated at London's White Swan with Ben Johnson, Christopher Marlowe and Shakespeare in 1580.

They're all brilliant, extraordinary geniuses; I am colourless, ordinary, without a streak of genius. To them, I am bereft of wit, an unoccupied place on the seat.

I would be content to feel I'm there, even just physically. If only he would touch me, lay his hand on my shoulder. I'd like him to be proud of me. I wish they would all disappear, so that we might be alone, so that I might kiss his mouth as he speaks, as he laughs, as he turns his face towards the others.

Picassiette tells us that the other day, as he was looking out the window of his studio in rue La Boétie, he saw a woman kiss the trashcan in front of his building.

Laughing at this, Jean adds that Maurice Sachs has admitted to him that he gets down on his knees in front of a photograph of Jean every morning. A needle of jealousy starts knitting my guts.

André Read looks suddenly prematurely old. I'm delighted to see that Colette and Max Ernst look as jealous as I am.

They all end up leaving. Picasso shakes my hand, turning his head to look at Max Jacob. Colette looks at me with a vaguely bored expression. Max Jacob grants me a compassionate smile and Jean squeezes my arm with an air of embarrassment. We go our separate ways.

Not knowing where to go now that my dear mother thinks I'm in Switzerland, I return to sleep on the bridge. The snow has almost melted and the temperature has gone up, but it's still quite cold. I take out my spare set of clothes and put them on, piece by piece.

Ten minutes later, I'm as round as a fellow made of fabric. I lie down as comfortably as possible, using my tweed overcoat as a pillow and fall asleep straight away.

Throughout the night, strange patrons walk past me. To begin with, an old lady. She rummages lengthily in her pocket and takes out an agate marble which she deposits in my hat on the ground. A man dressed all in black approaches me, taking a knife out of his pocket. I'm terrified of being pierced by him, but he lets it fall, tip first into the hat.

As soon as he leaves, an old man steps forward, his palms pressed together. I wonder what he has in store for me. He puts his hands into the hat and when I peer inside, I find a dead grasshopper between the marble and the knife.

A little boy hops up, stops short, undoes his fly and passes water lengthily into my headgear. I stare at him, stunned. Just at that moment a teenage girl with ruffled hair steps out of nowhere. She bends over on the instant to undo her corset and proffer her breast. I suck

in the milk thus offered in great gulps for a
few minutes, but she abruptly withdraws, all
affrighted, and races off as if she were being
followed.

Max Jacob (I think it's him) moves forward
very slowly now, as if he's half-dead. He takes
a Star of David made of yellow fabric out of his
pocket and casts it onto my midriff.

Jean arrives right behind him, slips a whole
butterfly under my eyelid and takes off hand in
hand with Max Jacob who has in the meantime
changed into Maurice Sachs, Max Ernst being
only one of his many avatars.

Tiresias is there, suddenly before me. He
proffers his thumb for me to suck. Then he
throws me a set of completely rusty keys.
The young woman I met the other day (it's
definitely her) runs past again. She realizes that
I'm the one she's fleeing and scampers off. Just
before she disappears, she turns around to shout
that her name is Ludmilla. I knew that already, I
have no idea how.

The black-clad man comes back in turn,
squats down before me, dips his gloved hand
in a black, unbelievably deep pocket and ends
up pulling out a long blue cloud. With his
other hand, he forces me to open my mouth
and pushes the whole cloud slowly inside it,
as if there was no hurry at all. When I wake up
next morning, the hat is empty. Everything has
disappeared.

The Blade

XIII

"You there already? I wasn't expecting you before eight o'clock."

"Yes, I slept here. I had nowhere to go."

"Cocteau didn't keep you?"

"He, uh ... I think he was ashamed of me."

"I doubt it. You're imagining things. What's that hangdog look? You have to believe in yourself, by God! You're going to be pleased. I'd like to suggest a bit of action. You're going to be the passer-by this time. I suggest that to begin with—to get into the swing of it—you ask your way of every young woman who catches your attention. Your priority will be to choose the most exquisite ones. Pretend to be Swiss or— why not—an English tourist, since you speak the language fluently. Secondly, after an hour of warm up, you'll invite one of them for a cup of coffee."

"You can't do that kind of thing. You know that very well. They'll never agree."

"Don't be so sure. Women love direct men, men who know what they want. Despite appear-

ances, they're actually very fond of breaking
conventions. Come, let's take a walk on the
Champs-Elysées—the best place for that kind of
thing."

The warm-up Tiresias has prepared goes
without a hitch. I bumble a little at the start
but manage to lock eyes with the most dazzling
beauties of Paris for several seconds in a row,
which makes a great impression on me. I'm
almost more afraid of my new-found audacity
than I am of the women themselves.

But when it's time to move on to the next
level, my gaze loses its balance and slithers onto
my shoes. A large banana lodges itself in my
airways. The first two young women I walk up to
look at me with disdain—which wreaks havoc
with my composure for the rest of the exercise.

Six rejections later, the banana in my voice
box has doubled in size.

With a heavy heart, I go and find Tiresias
who has hidden behind a tree to give me
support (thanks, Tiresias).

Chiding, he stands in front of me to massage
the muscles of my throat with his thumb and
index finger as if he wants to choke me. A few
minutes later, he sends me back to the market-
place so I can sell my squashed fruit to the first
lady buyer.

Seven attempts later (oh how much terror
and banana combined), a slightly horsey young

woman with a feathery hat agrees to come and take a café-crème by my side, out of compassion and because she seems to find me comical.

We sit at a table in Chez Marcel. Sitting down, she contemplates me with the look of a spectator awaiting a burlesque play. She doesn't say a word, seemingly waiting for me to perform, as if I was about to provide circus entertainment.

Just as I'm about to utter a few words, the whole banana slips into one of my lungs. I choke right in front of her, coughing and spitting out bits of pulp onto her cape.

She cleans her pelisse, barely repressing her disgust, staring at my jaw as if it's a sewer.

The conversation goes from one topic to another without dwelling on any one subject (which is an obvious sign that it's not going to last). I find her more and more mannish; she finds me more and more common and witless. We are made to avoid each other. She ceases to make any effort whatsoever to keep the conversation afloat: one after the other, I see the last sentences die at my feet.

We make haste to withdraw from the unfortunate encounter. My spirits floundering in the deep, I head off in search of Tiresias.

Depressed by my account, he concedes that he has embarked a bit too hastily on my course of social and sentimental education. It doesn't matter, he says, we'll try something else. That's when I confide I think I'm in love with Jean and that I'm not up to any more conquest.

His face darkens but he keeps his counsel.

Tiresias has to go about his business, the nature of which is never specified. I find myself alone again, without any directives for the day. I don't know if he's forgotten. Has he done it on purpose? In any case, I don't feel like going back to beg. The very thought of it makes me queasy. This bridge is a suspended world. I remain here as if levitating between the river of the dead and the bank of the living.

I decide to leave limbo. I will do as I please today. The problem is that the thing I long for is also the thing that terrifies me the most.

I steel my nerves, telling myself that a little extra terror won't make a difference. I allow my yearning to turn me into someone else. I decide to give it free reign. Once the decision is taken, a kind of unsticking occurs in my mind. I come apart from myself. I decide to no longer be me, allowing desire to transform me. It's done. I am no longer myself. I am my desire.

It's even more terrifying than that: I am changing into the very object of my own desire. Today, for the first time entirely, I am no longer Thomas Hearse, born on the 1st of January 1913 in Brighton; I am Jean Cocteau, born in Maisons-Laffitte on the 5th of July, 1889.

Now that I finally know who I am, I find myself infinitely more courageous. I feel my wings grow. I head for home, floating above the footpath towards the Madeleine-Palace Hôtel. I only hope that I will be at home when I get there.

I go down rue Tronchet, Trench Street more like — it's not worthy to open out onto the temple of the Madeleine and its high priest.

Here's the temple. The statue of Saint Luke is still decapitated. The Heurtebise lift is still out of order. I ascend the stairs, turning my back on the porter's protestations. No idea why he's vociferating, I have to go up one way or the other. I experience a little pleasure nevertheless listening to him complain in my absence.

Seven stories to climb. To get to the end of this staircase you need to be both besotted and a gifted mountain climber. I'm obliged to pause on the sixth floor to catch my breath. Not abnormal for someone in my state. I've been forty-four for several minutes now: that's twenty-five more than usual. I just have to get used to it.

I knock at the door, all emotional at the idea of seeing myself, but I don't answer. I must not be home. I tell myself I must be at Colette's or Picasso's. I can be so worldly at times.

Mechanically, I turn the handle. The door opens. I enter the darkness of my temple. The tang of opium hangs heavy in the air. The open

door of the restroom holds back a flow of light.
I open the dam and find myself in the comfy
intimacy of my water closet. Three of my hairs
await me in the ivory sink. Removing these
hairy arabesques, I place them carefully in my
wallet to collect them.

Through the window, I spot a man crossing
the street to enter the hotel. It's the other me.
There I am entering my home again. All the
same, I'm a bit surprised I'm coming back so
unexpectedly. Which is why I decide to meet
myself on the staircase.

From the top of the winding stair, I observe
my hat ascending in a spiral. Like me, I pause
on the sixth floor to catch my breath. My other
self is forty-four years old as well. When I reach
the seventh floor, I stare at myself in surprise:

"Mr Butterfly! There you are in my place
before me. Are you not with Tiresias?"

"He left without giving marching orders."

"I see, well, you might as well come in while
you're waiting. To what do I owe the pleasure
of your presence?"

My second self's throat chokes up inexplicably. Unable to utter a word, I stretch forth
my hand towards the other me. I'm so moved
that instead of placing my hand on my neck, I
put my hand around my other self's throat. The
other me also places his hand on my throat. We
stay there holding each other for a few moments
without saying a word, like two men trying to

gently strangle each other on the stair.

I feel the other me's pulse beating against my thumb; the palm at my throat holds my Adam's apple like a piece of fruit.

A longer fruit instantly starts to grow in the second me's pants.

My other's me's pants is germinating fully. The hand on one of my Adam's apples goes down on the two hidden stems, unclasping their covers. It holds them tightly one against the other like a bouquet of tulips.

That's when an extraordinary thing occurs.

My other me kneels down and starts to take my stem in his mouth. In only a few short seconds, the white venom runs over in my throat in little spurts. I choke voluptuously as I swallow the beverage.

Over the following months, we make love several times a week. But it's never enough to fill the breach. I would like him to be in me all the time. I would like to be no more than the extension of his member, but he is always busy, always elsewhere, ever absent. I spend entire days awaiting him.

I am but the shadow of Jean Cocteau, a shadow he undoes at will, letting it fall on the armchair like a creased garment. Sometimes, when he returns alone, he agrees to yoke himself to his shadow for a few hours, the night.

When boredom and waiting overwhelm me,

I join Tiresias so he can give me some loopy
task to fulfil.

Sometimes, it's writing tasks, at other times
it's begging or absurd labours whose aim is
to place me in the most embarrassing situations. These exercises have no doubt a certain
efficacy as I stammer less and less and manage
to control my emotions for the most part. But
I carry out orders without acquiring a taste for
them, without taking pleasure in my progress. I
only feel whole when he's inside me.

The worst of all is when I've been waiting
for him for hours and he comes back with some
new neophyte in the process of developing
artistic talent. There is nothing that Jean loves
more than a young man whose talents have yet
to blossom.

He makes these young minds hatch in front
of me. I stay quietly in my place, a useless
midwife next to the doctor. He listens to them,
corrects their dullest literary efforts, counsels
them, rocks them in his arms, encouraging. He
writes letters to them by the dozen. Mostly, he
brings home a horde of admirers: Jean resides
in his throne on the bed, sitting with his legs
crossed. For hours, he sews the eyes of his
open-mouthed nurslings. He weaves his spider's
web and we are happy to surrender.

I'm being unfair, of course. There's nothing
predatory about Jean. I'm the one who is

throwing myself at his feet, begging him to devour me. In the end, what hurts the most is his refusal to swallow me up. I'd like him to be a boa constrictor, for him to swallow me whole in one single gulp.

When they finally leave (there's always one who persists, one I have to frighten off with my stare), I beseech Jean to slip me on like an old sock. I ask him to slide into me for hours, to fill me with seed.

When he smokes too much, he is incapable of doing this. As the opium makes him impotent, I stay awake all night watching him sleep. I've sometimes hidden his little balls of opium so he can't smoke them, so he can perforate my body far into the night.

I watch him exhaust himself in me, egging him on when he starts to flag in the small hours of the morning. He resembles a man trudging over endless fields of snow.

I feel he is tormented by something. He tells me about his existential anxieties. His eyes often cloud over when he peers at me. I get the feeling he's looking for something within me that I cannot offer. He feels cut off. You can see it in his eyes.

He sometimes tells me that I'm the son he never had. At other times, he calls me his young monster.

After we couple, he stares at me for a few seconds. His eyes still aglow, his face soaked in

sweat, he bursts out laughing from the effort of
the ride. His pupils remain warm and dilated.
Then they slowly diminish, especially after an
opium pipe. My heart contracts when I see the
precious gleam disappear in the dark sink of his
pupils.

When we lock eyes, I watch out for the
slightest sagging in his pupils, living at the
mercy of those small black suns. I try to pull
him towards me, but he remains anchored, far
away on the horizon. Even when he's inside me,
there are times when I feel he's distant, as if he
is merely mechanically dipping his quill in the
inkwell of my body.

Then I tell myself I might have to stab him
to feel close, really inside him. Stick a blade
into his belly, like an umbilical cord tying us
together. Only then might I really feel him
vibrate, his face entirely lost in mine, his gaze
open at last.

Now that I've finally experienced real
intimacy, I feel close to no one.

When he leaves, I press my naked body
against the window to watch him go. He turns
around in the street as soon as he reaches the
opposite pavement, not to blow love towards me
but to make me understand with an exasperated
gesture that he doesn't want me to display
myself in this way, naked at the window. He
says we could end up facing a prison sentence. I
retort that I dream of finding myself alone with

him in a cell for a lifetime. He answers briskly
that that is indeed an unfulfillable dream that
he hopes will not come true in any way. A fallen
Samson, I gaze on weakly at the granite pillars
of the temple of the Madeleine, concealing my
genitals.

In this room, Jean corrected the final proofs
of *The Holy Terrors*. I see the ghosts of Paul and
Elisabeth sitting on the bed. Patiently, they look
at me. Jean was exactly my age when he thought
of the idea. He says it took him another twenty
years to dare to put pen to paper. Written in
seventeen days in a clinic. Perhaps I would need
that kind of place ...

Rarely does he agree to let us leave together.
He does not wish our bond to be visible to the
public eye.

There are times when he spends the whole
morning in my company. We remain nude or
swathed in the hotel's white bathing robes.
Smoking his pipe, he refuses to let me taste his
opium. He has qualms about having introduced
quite a few to the drug without realizing the
consequences. Not that it bothers me. I prefer to
inhale the smoke that has already been through
his lungs.

Blades of opium sear my throat, stinging my
nostrils and eyes. The smoke spreads through
the room in thick coils, impalpable embroidery
that binds itself into script before loosening into

drawing. An immense white beard levitating above the bed. The air is quite unbreathable, but I like it that way.

I make sure he does everything with me when he's there. I want to occupy every position, invest every object around him. I wish to become everything, to become indispensable. When he takes his coffee, I offer myself as a tray for his use. Although he is a little unwilling, I make him deposit his hot coffee spoon on my belly so a black tear spills into the drain of my navel.

I insist so heavily on being used as a writing desk that he finally gives in to the request. He writes the whole last section of *The Infernal Machine* on my back. I give him the rhythm of the writing with each minute coming and going of his nestled member lodged between my buttocks. He reads all the lines aloud. When I sense the end is nigh, I abruptly stop the metronome to indicate that he is to come to a climax only when he reaches the very last line of the play. He complies until the close. The red scarf is tied around the incestuous Jocasta's neck. When she hangs herself, he lays his hand on my Adam's apple and in one last unbridled cavalcade he empties himself of all the rest.

At the onset of spring, the play is complete, composed, recomposed, wrapped up, sent off and published. Smoking far too many pipes,

Jean no longer wishes to write. To distract him, to bring him back to life, I ask him to write on my skin. In Indian ink, with a brush, he scrawls wispy scrolls on me, stars, fish, horses, strangely mysterious, frightening figures. His drawings tighten into script only to be released into long undulating lines. I would love to keep all these scrawls indefinitely but the ink never stays on me for very long, my skin erases and blurs it. My pores drink the ink like a sponge.

He draws a star on my brow one day, telling me I am his little golem, that he endows me with life by dint of this sign. I answer that I am his creation. Indeed, he retorts, but you are free to leave. I take it badly and throw a jealous tantrum. When Cocteau senses a storm brewing, he lowers his head and stays silent. I see that he is bending more and more under the burden that I have become. He says that he is as free as I am bound.

It's time to put an end to Cocteau.

XIV

I find myself alone in the bedroom. As is
his wont, Cocteau locks himself every morning
into the bathroom to perform his ablutions.
Through the door, I listen to the music of the
water flowing over his body. I look around this
bachelor pad of a hotel room, now a chamber of
torment.

Placed on the window sill is Jean's
cane-sword.

There it is, laid out for my use: the crime
weapon.

I hold the sheath in my hands and pull
out the sword. The blade is sharp, pointy
and cutting, designed to pierce as deeply as
possible. I thrust it into the bed, perforating the
eiderdown. A cloud of white feathers puffs out.

I stick the tip of the sword into the quilt
again and continue pushing until the bed is
impaled. Meeting a certain resistance, the
blade slowly sinks into the tender flesh of the
mattress, piercing it through to the bones. I hear
the muted squeaking of the blade as it grates

against the springs. Playing it like a violin, I come and go with the implacable blade.

I withdraw it slowly from the entrails of the mattress. I brandish and thrust it, impaling the fat of the air.

I move agitatedly through the room and shove the tip of the sword into the gap between two drawers. The drawer squeaks a little and comes loose. I pull it ajar with my fingers.

At the bottom there's a package wrapped in newspaper where a large headline reads "ONE OF LANDRU'S VICTIMS?", followed by smaller print: "A skeleton has been found in Clichy, buried under the foundations of a building in the rue de Paris, next door to Landru's former lodgings. The coincidence has roused public opinion".

I undo the wrapping and find three green, slightly yellowed balls inside. The poet's drug. The poppy capsules from which Cocteau derives the paste which he smokes, his noxious substance.

I pick out one of the balls and examine it closely. It's the size of a small green tomato. Hard as a stone. I place the ovary of the poppy against the sword and draw it carefully down the blade, pressing down. A whitish liquid instantly seeps out. Opium milk.

I put the extruded tear to my mouth and lick it. The taste is disgustingly acrid. Holding the capsule over my wide-open mouth, I squeeze

the ovary and let the milk drop from the tiny
little breast into my mouth.

I swallow down quickly to avoid the acidu-
lated aftertaste, the poet's white blood.

As soon as the rind is empty, I send a
probing tongue deep into the cut and throw
the empty husk under the bed. I close the
newspaper with the two remaining capsules and
shove them into the drawer.

Just a few minutes later, I'm seized by a
strange exaltation. A feeling so strong I could
leap out the window. I feel like tearing everything apart, including the wallpaper. The water
is still gushing down behind the door. I hear it
flow with the power of a waterfall in full spate.

"You could barge into the bathroom ..."

"I suppose I could."

"You could blindly plunge the sword
through the shower curtain ..."

"I can already picture the stream of blood
flowing down the curtain. The resistance of the
flesh to begin with, the shudder of the body, the
spasms ..."

"When he collapses, you can just slip out the
door."

"They'll know it was me."

"You can always say you thought you
were fighting off an intruder. An accident. You
thought Cocteau was at the opera. You didn't
know that Polonius was standing hapless
behind the curtain."

"It won't stand up to scrutiny. Besides, I'm not sure what you're saying."

"I'm projecting my thoughts onto you. I shouldn't have intervened."

"Where are you? Who are you?"

"I'd better not say any more. Let's just put this conversation down to the hallucinogenic effect of the opium."

"I don't want to hear you anymore!"

"Understood. I'll let you finish."

When he finally comes out of the bathroom, surrounded by a thick cloud of vapour and opium, I'm still under the influence of the opioid. I can tell by the look in his eyes that he has been smoking on the sly. I sit up straight in the bed, still beside myself with anger. The warm cutting blade slumbers under my thigh.

The man in the bathrobe is just jabbering. He looks agitated. These last few days, he's been trying to quit smoking. He talks of nothing else without making the slightest effort to stop. I hear his words, but I don't understand what he's talking about. His mouth moves, producing the usual sounds. He looks at me with his little piercing eyes. His eyebrows rise to the side like two caterpillars incapable of touching. The caterpillars rise up to assault each other, their defenceless little legs squirm on the stage of his brow. He speaks without expecting an answer, as if he's alone in the bedroom.

"When deprived of opium, I get cold, I catch colds. I cease to be hungry. I'm anxious to impose my inventions. As a smoker, I feel warm, immune to colds. I experience the pangs of hunger, my impatience disappears."

He'll get a stab right in the middle of his heart. That will shut him up at last.

He looks out the window, the way he usually does.

I'll penetrate his heart from behind. I'll pierce it by driving it in through his back. He won't even notice. It'll be over in a second.

But he never ceases to natter, to blather on into the steam:

"Opium is a decision to be taken. Our mistake is to want to smoke and partake of the privileges of those who do not smoke."

I hunker down on the bed, ready to pounce when the time comes.

He keeps chattering, turning his head to look out the window from time to time, as if he was expecting someone of more importance.

The tip of the blade cuts into the back of my knee. I turn my head and spot a blood stain on the bed. He's talking to the window now. His back offers itself up.

"Alcohol provokes fits of madness. Opium provokes fits of wisdom."

Without the slightest noise, I rise, the sheath in my hidden hand, the weapon in the other. I press myself against him.

Slowly, he sighs, feeling the touch of my chest against his back. He lets his head loll back onto my shoulder.

"People always talk about the enslavement of opium. Of course, the regularity of the hours it imposes requires discipline, but it also offers freedom. Freedom from visits, from the circles of seated people. The luxury of opium, its rituals, reassure me. It's an exquisite variety of poison."

His throat is clear. Instead of roaring out laughing, he sighs a full-throated sigh. The veins in his neck bulge and stick out.

"We all carry within us a thing folded inwards, like those wooden Japanese flowers that open up in water. In truth, none of us possesses the same kind of flower … It's quite possible that people who don't smoke will never discover the kind of flower that opium would have unrolled inside them."

The grain of his skin. Turkey neck. His throat just asking to be slit, putting a stop to that endless succession of phrases. One brisk and brutal gesture will do the trick. Something horrid is pushing me to do this. An obscure, incomprehensible force.

I feel like howling a hunting call. To put this creature to death. You're going to do it now.

"I owe opium my finest hours. I prefer an artificially-induced sense of balance than no balance at all."

I experience a moment of intense drowsiness all of a sudden. Combined with dizziness. My hand grips the pommel of the sword.

My exaltation subsides. I feel myself falling into a state of near-catalepsy.

"Before I take my opium at the usual hour of eleven in the morning, nothing else exists ..."

Without making the slightest noise, with extreme care, I pull out the blade. I ready myself to deal a quick blow directly into his throat.

With both arms extended behind me, I feel like an angel.

The dark angel of death.

A terrible strength takes hold of my arm. I have no idea where it comes from.

I imagine the blows dealt by the cutting edge of the blade. Sharp deadly lashes that sink in deep as the hacking of an axe on his throat and chest. The blood oozes at first only to gush out in little regurgitated mouthfuls. The dumbstruck look on his face.

"After a smoke of opium, the body starts to think. But not in the confused manner of Descartes. The body meditates, it dreams, the body soars. The smoker considers himself flying from above ... It's all a question of speed. Motionless speed. The speed of the self. Opium is the speed of silk."

"Puns are a pain."

"Nice rejoinder, my butterfly. You're making steady progress."

He hasn't noticed a thing.

He pursues his day-dreams, blathering on endlessly out loud to himself.

A lamb to the slaughter.

But I drop my wings abruptly, entirely discouraged.

I reposition the point of the blade at the lip of the sheath.

I push it soundlessly into the velvety casing.

"Doctors are adamant that opium dulls the senses, depriving us of our values. But although opium pulls the old scale of values from under our feet, it sets up another one in its stead that's far taller and finer."

I'm not going to be able to kill him.

"The patience of the poppy. Once a smoker, always a smoker. Opium knows how to bide its time. The soul-destroying boredom of the cured smoker. Everything you do in life, even making love, is done on the express train that shuttles towards death. To smoke opium is to jump off a speeding train; it's to go about other things than life and death ... Tamed, opium will soothe the evil of cities where trees die standing up ... Opium is a revolt."

I will wait until I love him less.

I hand the sheathed cane-sword to him, saying that we would do well to go outside for a breath of fresh air, that the unbreathable air in this room is simply suffocating. For once, he agrees, to humour me. He doesn't seem to realize how lucky he is.

We go out into the street. I feel an irresistible urge to hold his hand, but I know it's out of the question. Forbidden.

Sensing after an hour that he has had his fill of me, I mention a meeting with Tiresias as a pretext to get away. He smiles in relief and departs in a hurry. Perhaps he did sense something after all.

With a coffin floating around in my heart I go to see my friend Tiresias. The joy of seeing his hairy, furrowed old face lightens my torments a little. I would love to fall asleep in the huge pillow of his beard. He pulls a sorry face and holds me tight for an instant against his chest so I will tell him my misadventures.

I confess my attempted murder. His asymmetrical face is instantly plunged in rue.

After a long, thoughtful pause, he proposes the usual rite of passage which I am to accept, he adds, before knowing anything about it.

So I agree to the terms, more out of sympathy than conviction. That's when he reveals that I'll have to jump off Mirabeau Bridge and let myself be carried off by the Seine. I am on no account to latch onto anything, and I'm not allowed to try to reach the banks of the river. When I ask him how I'm supposed to get out of a sticky situation like that, he answers he doesn't know any better than I do. I have to keep an open mind and keep my wits about me.

A little flustered all the same, I protest that the ordeal is too perilous and I don't want to die trying. He answers that in some ancient tribes the initiated are subjected to bloody trials that are infinitely more perilous. He asks me if I would rather have a few teeth knocked out with a hammer and chisel, like young men from the Murring tribe in Australia.

Scarcely an hour later, I find myself atop the bridge, contemplating the silky reflections of my figure in the water. Under Mirabeau Bridge flows the sanies. I have in any case nothing to lose.

Taking a deep breath, my legs all atremble, I leap out over the water.

The drop down to the vast liquid body is endless.

The water suddenly slaps into my face and I sink to the bottom of the river like an aspirin. The temperature of the water works its way into my body, paralysing my chest.

My lungs fill. I cough out the contents at the surface. Tiresias is nowhere to be seen on the bridge. I experience the greatest difficulty in keeping my head above water. Too late, I realize he must want me to drown, to free Cocteau, to remove the thorn from his foot.

Despite my attempts at swimming, I start to go numb. The water is even more glacial than I anticipated but I'm almost insensitive to the cold. I'm just having awful trouble breathing. Even with my mouth above the waterline, the liquid mass compresses my torso, the Seine's black scarf pulled tightly around me.

I drift on and on. My face, my thoughts numbing. I can no longer feel a thing and am close to falling asleep.

I sense myself receding, gently rocked by the watered fabric of the river. Only the features of my face remain above water. I'm nothing more than a floating face. A mortuary mask.

Suddenly, I feel pushed about by something hard. In my semi-somnolence, I tell myself a large fish is testing my flesh, nudging me with its nose.

The fish presses up against me, pushing into my ribs. I grasp it with a weak hand: it's small, thin and long.

It isn't a fish. It's a perch.

At the other end of the stick is Tiresias.

XV

"The doctors say you contracted pneumonia and that it could have gone awry."

"Just pneumonia?"

"They say you have a very good chance of convalescing, given enough rest. You should be proud of yourself, you know that? You survived the ordeal."

"When will I be able to leave?"

"To avoid risking a relapse, you have to stay another week, at the very least."

"A week! I've been here for weeks already."

"I know. I'm sorry. I didn't think you were that weak. I thought about drowning, numbness, obstacles in the water, but I never considered pneumonia."

"What about Jean, what's he up to? Did he come to see me much?"

"He's very busy at the moment. He's on the point of leaving for Vevey in Switzerland. You'll be out by the time he gets back. He'll only be staying in Vevey for ten days or so."

Lying on the bed, I find a photograph of
Jean on a horse. He has drawn on the photo,
as usual. The horse sports a large star in its
eye. Behind Jean on horseback, a young man
appears, drawn in faint ghostly lines, consumed
by his own flames. He's reciting, his arm raised.
An ardent young man.

Jean's room is lukewarm now, as if appeased
after a very high temperature. The temple
behind the window seems to be coming back to
life with the trees.

Jean is to return in three days. All I have
to do is wait and try to be reasonable. My
feverish hunger for him has evaporated with the
sickness. I can't even feel my erstwhile shyness.
All I have left is a tender desire to hold him in
my arms without expecting requited feelings.

I look at the photograph and the drawing
he has done of me. My former self now feels
ridiculous. I don't think there's an intended
caricature of me in the drawing, but I suddenly
find myself stupid, antiquated, anachronistic.
Perhaps that's what he wanted to suggest by
drawing me dressed in an ancient Greek toga.
By contrast, Jean is dressed in trendy modern
clothes. He's opaque, tangible, a man of his
time. As for me, I'm transparent, ghostly, a relic
of the past. A little noble, certainly, but more
than a little ludicrous. The horse of his thoughts
carries him far away from me.

I tear up the photograph and throw the pieces into the bin.

Jean's belongings are still there in his drawers. They still entice me as much as they used to. I feel like shredding the photos of his erstwhile heartthrob Raymond Radiguet. Jean Desbordes's drawings too. My eye alights on a book left lying haphazardly on top of the books on his shelf. I open it out and there is Jean's sinuous calligraphy snaking about, accompanied by a set of little drawings. It isn't a novel, it's a diary.

I can feel the temperature of my face rising like a gaslight. At last, I hold in my hands Jean's most secret thoughts. Suddenly, I'm scared. Scared that he'll catch me red-handed, with my fingers stuck in the book. Scared to find out that he no longer loves me, scared he only loves me a little. I rush over to lock the door, even though he isn't supposed to come back before the day after tomorrow.

Frantically, I flick through the intimate logbook in search of the date of our first encounter.

But on the 30th of January there's nothing. 1932. It's certainly the right year.

Just "Call Geneviève about the article." The following day is the same. Just "Geneviève!" There isn't a single mention of our most memorable experience in the cemetery of Montparnasse.

The following days are equally empty. I
don't get a single mention. It isn't as if there's
a paucity of names in here. I come across an
avalanche of different people called Jean: Jean
Auranche, Jean Bourgoint, Jean Desbordes,
Jean Hugo, Jean Le Roy, Jean Marécage, Jean
Wiener, Jean Aiassé and Jean Passe. You'd think
that in our glorious day and age everyone goes
by the name of Jean. And that's not counting
the names that I recognize more easily: Juan
Gris, Eluard, Braque, Colette, Chanel, Kisling,
Picassiette. I am not mentioned a single time. As
if I'd never existed. And thus I'm forced to come
to terms with the obvious fact that I have never
been anything more than one out of dozens of
nameless young admirers.

I flip to the last pages of the almanac and
fall flat on my back into the face of horror itself.
Proof of another loved one.

The first thing I see is a heart, drawn in a
slightly childish way around the letter N.

Nathan? Noel? Nicholas? Norbert? Nestor?
There aren't that many names that start with an
N …

I read: "Am in love AT LAST after all this
time." And on another page, without a shadow
of a doubt: "I'm finally going to be able to
forget Raymond." Then an N surrounded by a
heart shape and inscribed in calligraphic writing
again on three consecutive pages.

Then, "Departure for Vevey."

That N burns my retina. Negative, No, Null, Nowhere, Never. No survivors. Down in the netherworld, I unlock the door and leave the room with the diary in my hand.

I walk along the banks of the Seine, sobbing like a child. I hear my voice spitting out its usual pitch in jagged bursts. A surprisingly small voice. My tears start to hit the most high-pitched notes. I open the diary again, read the same names, the same sentences, pithy and murderous as the blades in a penknife.

Holding this thing between my hands is suddenly unbearable. I'm going to leave the notebook on the bank of the Seine. May somebody else find it, may a sweeper take it away. No, too uncertain. I'm going to throw it in the water. Jean will no doubt be furious. I no longer care.

I hold it for one last time in my hands.

With a grand gesture, like Dargelos, I throw the black snowball over the parapet. The dark rectangle falls like a slaughtered bird. It disappears into the water, failing to resurface.

XVI

"I don't know any Nicolas. I've never known any."

"Nathan, then. Norbert!"

"None. I don't know anyone called Nathan, and I don't know anyone called Norbert."

"So who's N, then?"

"I see you've been going through my things again. I hope for your sake you haven't taken any of my letters. They mean a lot to me and I would be very resentful."

"Letters too! So who is it then? Noel?"

"There's no Noel to speak of."

"Who is it?"

"You've looked through my diary. I knew I shouldn't have left it here. When I realized ... My goodness, Thomas, you're so difficult. You know very well I never promised you anything. I've never lied to you. I've never deceived you, never deluded you. I never told you I loved you!"

"You did."

"Yes, but I never said I was in love with you.

You know I often tell my friends I love them.
They know what to expect."

"You told me one day that Eros's arrow was
beginning to pierce your pants."

"That was just an image. Eros stands for
eroticism. Which doesn't necessarily mean
love."

"I was the more deceived."

"Don't look at me with those eyes, and stop
pretending you're a Shakespearean character.
You're hamming the part. Oh, come on, please
tell me you're not going to start crying again.
We can still see each other, embrace. Nathalie is
very understanding. She's very tolerant."

"Nathalie?"

"Yes … it's incredible, I've fallen in love
with a woman again. After all these years. I can
hardly believe my own heart. Madly in love
with a woman. She wishes us to marry. We
want to have children."

"A woman? "

"Nathalie Paley. Like you, she has partly
English origins. Marie-Laure introduced us
during the projection of *A Poet's Blood*. She's
only twenty-seven, but she doesn't find me too
old."

"I don't find you too old either."

"I know, my little one … You make me sad.
Please be happy for me. I'm starting to resus-
citate after Radiguet's death. She's offering me
another shot at life. A new heart."

"Nathalie Paley. Isn't that the princess everyone is talking about?"

"Yes, exactly! I would never have believed this could happen. She's Tsar Alexander's niece and the great duke Alexandrovitch's daughter. Her father and her brother were both killed by the Bolsheviks, but as you may know she was able to flee to Finland with her mother as a child. You could say she's a miraculously saved princess."

"When did you meet?"

"A few weeks ago. But I know now that she's the woman of my life."

"And the man of your life was Radiguet."

"Oh, come, my little one. Let's not be sullen. Let's go out, I need air. This room is making me claustrophobic."

Jean is in seventh heaven; I'm in hell. And yet, despite it all, I'd like him to be happy. Since we met, he's been pale and languid. His face looked like a dead leaf pressed between the pages of a book. Now that spring is here, the buds have burgeoned in his eyes again. With his red neck scarf, he looks like Aristide Bruant in the posters of Toulouse-Lautrec.

On Tiresias's good advice, Jean has suggested I embark on a voyage to distant lands. He wishes to offer me a journey to Indochina. Tiresias claims it's the best place for an initiatory quest.

I've had my fill of initiation. I've swallowed a Seine full of it. But Jean's insistence is such that I end up complying. He also wishes me to procure opium for him in one of the north-western provinces of Siam. In fact, I wonder if that isn't his main motivation, after the prospect of no longer being encumbered by me. But let us not be bitter, I still feel his affection. He adds that his usual suppliers in the Chinese quarter of Paris are no longer trustworthy. The quality of the opium they provide is poor.

I spend hours in discussion with my two mentors. Both shower me with advice, filling my pockets with fatherly goodwill. I am touched by one of Jean's expressions, a phrase that dominates all others. A key sentence that will stay embedded in me like the figurehead at the prow of a ship. He tells me that at the age of nineteen, Diaghilev, the famous Russian choreographer, issued a challenge to him that he has never forgotten since that day. Three words: "Surprise me, Jean".

He confesses not to want to make me feel the same pressure he had to endure, preferring to release me from the gaze of other people which he says has always cramped his style. Here is therefore its variant, which is also a way of pulling me out of him: "Thomas, surprise yourself."

XVII

Departure for Marseille.

The *Siam* leaves in ten days, which would give me enough time to prepare my journey, pack my suitcases and bid my farewells, but I prefer to avail of the *Ophelia* which leaves in only three days. A bit of a hasty departure but that's just as well. I don't want to have the leisure to think, to consider the risks of the voyage, practical matters, and end up going back on my decision. Better to sever the rope quickly. My mother believes I'm in Switzerland in any case.

As it's my first voyage and I'm required to embark on it alone, Tiresias prefers to drive me to the port in Marseille in the dilapidated, old Ford that Jean is lending us with an eagerness doubled by his guilt at not accompanying me himself.

"The automobile is capable of massaging organs that no masseur can reach. It's the only cure for disorder of the sympathetic nervous system."

"Thanks for your help, Jean. I'm really sorry about your almanac. I don't know what came over me ... and for the rest ..."

"Let's not talk about that anymore. Water under the bridge."

A miniature version of him comes up in the rear view mirror. He continues to shrink, waving one end of the red scarf wrapped round his neck. The scarf reminds me of Isodora Duncan's. Nothing but a red dot, and then it's gone.

The car breaks down several times on the road (burst tyres, dead bobbin, weak, almost non-existent brakes), which ends up irritating Tiresias to such a degree that he forgets to keep the conversation going (something which I used to find hard to imagine).

On several occasions, I'm tempted to ask him the burning question that I haven't dared to put to him since we met: what happened to his eye, that missing piece of face? But he's so grumpy because of our engine failures that I recoil from broaching such a sensitive subject. I settle for observing him from time to time. With the empty socket hidden from sight, he's actually rather handsome. I don't find him bland at all. Between gear shifts, he lays his hand on the pommel of his cane-sword as if holding a sceptre, with an air of supreme authority. If the right side of his face lends him some august nobility, the left side remains

an enigma. An impenetrable, stitched up eye,
closed for evermore.

In spite of everything, we get to our destination safe and sound a few hours before the
Ophelia departs. I have my passport and ticket
in hand; all I have left to do is to take my leave
of Tiresias. He suddenly looks moved and
embraces me a little too roughly. He hands me
a notebook bound in suede, instructing me to
start it as soon as I feel the urge to write.

I embrace him one last time and allow
myself to be swallowed up by the ocean liner's
white mouth. I climb up onto the gigantic upper
deck where the seamen are setting up a game of
shuffleboards.

I spot Tiresias in the crowd thronged below.
His usual imposing stature has shrunk to a
speck. From my vantage point, he's almost as
small as the other family men in the crowd.
He waves his arms and cups his hands in the
shape of a bullhorn to shout words that the cold
wind douses in the waves. My own words are
devoured by the cries of the gulls. We settle for
sign-language.

The immense ship recedes like an iceberg.

Stowed inside the *Ophelia*, I head off in
search of my cabin and end up turning round
in circles at the bottom of an endless maze of
identical corridors.

When I finally manage to locate the right corridor, I realize I don't have the key to the dungeon that would allow me to gain access to the unfindable cabin. If I had pebbles at hand, I would sow them on the floor to find my way the next time round, but the iceberg is a white forest devoid of pebbles. And so I return to the surface to withdraw my key, but the thought of going back down again only to climb back up combines with the rolling motion of the boat, making me more and more nauseous.

I'm forced to sit down in the ship's restaurant where a group of jubilant French people take pity of my paleness and exhort me to join them with many a cry. They put a thousand questions to me without seeming to realize that I'm seasick, an oversight which my stomach decides to let them know about all of a sudden when it regurgitates my lunch onto the ankle boots of the more reserved lady at my side, a certain Raphaëlle de Veauregard, a high-ranking professor who holds the Chair for Oriental languages at the University of Lyon.

Her companion, who is a little less splattered, but just as delighted to have the leisure of inspecting the contents of my stomach on his trousers and his silk stocking, goes by the name of Mr. Mortel (a member of the group who is so respectable he doesn't seem to have a first name). He's Dean of the Humanities at the Ancient Sorbonne. His face sports a ginger, diseased-looking beard. To allege that it is a piss-coloured beard that sullies his face would be inexact. The beard evokes a spray of vomit coagulated in mid-flight as it came in contact with the air. His face and his sock are now no longer mismatched.

Nevertheless, he considers me with the eyes of one who has just experienced the assaults of an overlarge suppository. The worst affront he ever received.

Raphaëlle de Veauregard starts to graze the edge of her lips a little, baring her bovine dentures. There's something old-fashioned about her eyes. The erudite couple bears a grudge for the rest of the cruise because of this incident.

By contrast, the other members of the assembly are full of concern; they cosset and nurse me and come up with medication in record time. Being the youngest in the group, I'm pampered by a whole swarm of humming nannies. Madame Barbero offers her grandmotherly advice, Madame Falk makes me sniff her smelling salts. Madame Lisbeth Long, a Swede with Chinese origins, bestows her massages on me, giving my big toe a hard pinch, a toe that is apparently connected to the stomach. In her care, I end up having a sore toe as well as being seasick, but her heart is in the right place.

In spite of their ministrations, I remain queasy for the duration of the crossing. For

close to a month, I'm forced to spend a good
part of the day in a semi-recumbent position to
avoid throwing up. Curled up in a nest of silken
cushions, I listen in on the worldly conversa-
tions of my new foster family.

While most of them wander around the
ship, I remain in the company of a grouchy old
hen, a retired primary-school teacher who goes
by the name of Madame Adolfine Hackette.
Casting condescending smirks at me, she pecks
complacently in her plate. I sometimes have the
(perhaps false) impression that she would like
to peck my eye with her beak.

Always retiring, there's the beautiful Camille
Aude, daughter of a diplomat. According to
the other passengers, they are both about to
settle in the Cambodian capital. Unfortunately,
we scarcely have the pleasure of sharing her
thoughts as she always stays slightly apart
from the group. She speaks even less than I do
(a prodigious feat in itself) and she seems to
be reading the complete works of Alexandre
Dumas (no mean task). We are practically all
in love with Camille Aude, but no one dares to
disturb her before she finishes reading *Queen
Margot*, the interminable *The Queen's Necklace*,
half a dozen musketeers, *Twenty Years Later*. I
begin to despise Dumas, particularly for his
prolific output: when she finishes reading one
of those chunky rectangular, one-thousand-page
blocks, she takes herself down to her cabin only

to settle in the restaurant again with another leather-bound doorstop in her hands. You get the impression that Dumas's office along with the office of his industrial collaborators are gathered together in Mademoiselle Aude's cabin.

Anyway, she holds her sway over me, despite her books (to think that up to now a woman reading represented the height of beauty to me). I settle for deciphering out of the corner of my eye the fleeting expressions that pass over her traits for an instant of bookish emotion, for a chuckle, a moment of suspense. She carries on reading, her head slightly inclined as if to capture the sound of Alexandre's voice.

I've tried, on several occasions, to get her attention but she only raises her head to cast a quick look at the sea between chapters. My shyness has forsaken me for once. My seasickness dissolves what little inhibition I have left. I've begun to experience a kind of salutary detachment towards everything, including myself.

This distance with regard to human relation-ships has triggered a feeling of profound apathy in me. I'm still in love with Jean but I don't care about him anymore; I'm on the point of falling in love with the beautiful reader without conceiving the slightest desire to approach her. The mere idea of having to get up and walk to her table and having to hold a conversation, even a monosyllabic one, increases my nausea.

I only feel well when I'm completely laid
out in my cabin, but staying in the hold plunges
me into such depths of boredom that I prefer to
climb up to the restaurant for a few hours a day,
despite the fact that Camille Aude's book-de-
vouring ends up making me feel even queasier.
Doing some reading of my own has become as
unbearable as eating.

After almost a month of pitching and rolling,
of vomiting and nausea, we finally reach the
port of Bangkok. For five days of dry land, the
ground moves under my feet as if I am still out
at sea. After the third day of stormy ground, I
start to wonder if I haven't forfeited my land
legs after having lost my sea legs during the
crossing.

Thankfully, my fear begins to fade, making
way for new kinds of unpleasantness in which
the stifling, clammy heat is not the least. When
the ocean winds cease to blow, the Asian
climate intervenes to put a definite end to all
attempts at breathing. It stuffs and fertilizes
your lungs in such a way that you are given the
instant impression that a kind of succulent plant
has started to grow at the bottom of your lungs.

As soon as we disembark, we each rush off
in the direction of our respective hotels. We
bid our rather brief fare-thee-wells: everyone
is relieved to be able to flee so much forced
intimacy. Like convalescing patients, we leave

our floating hospital and its interns without a flicker of regret. I have to endure a few more lame jokes from the menfolk in our company regarding my brilliant future as an ocean explorer. The benevolent ladies caress my cheek one last time. Adolfine Hackette's beak squints wistfully in the direction of my eye. She gives me a last sanctimonious smile. Mr Aude, Camille and Alexandre Dumas have already disappeared into the Bangkokian crowd.

The Mirror

XVIII

Before disembarking from the *Ophelia*, when the waves started to settle, I took myself out to the reception desk to look up the origin of the word "astonish" in the dictionary on board, the wondrously comforting *Petit Littré*.

"To cause a moral shock", it said, "from the Latin *extonare*, to cause to shake under the effect of thunder."

According to Jean, to astonish myself I am to give myself a shot of lightning.

Baudelaire used to define dandyism as "the pleasure of causing surprise coupled to the proud satisfaction of never being surprised." I am going to have to become a kind of anti-dandy, to allow myself to be surprised by everything, including myself.

Here I am now in my hotel room.

When I sit, the bed also sways and moves under my body. As soon as I put my foot back on the road, I'll feel obliged to surprise myself. The search for thunder will start to rumble in my head. The valiant knight that I am to become will be summoned to go off in search of his new self.

I lie on the bed to calm the dizziness and consider the best course of action. I am to turn myself into that which I am not, to do things that I would never ordinarily do. All my usual reflexes will have to be inverted. Something which, all things considered, feels like having to bend my knee backwards, against the joint. This new location will perhaps make the exercise feasible. It will no doubt be easier to shed my skin in a new place where no one knows me, where most objects and my surroundings remain foreign.

I can't even speak the language of the country, and the Siamese people's knowledge of English remains rudimentary at best. The little instinctive shyness left in me abated as soon as I sensed that speech would no longer be the main form of communication for me in this place. Words no longer have to clear a path through the tunnel of my throat, which means that the muscles of my neck are almost entirely relaxed.

It's time to go out. I've decided to head in the direction of the floating markets.

I'm in the canal district in no time, an apparently deserted area where a pack of ghostly dogs sway nevertheless, almost transparent they're so scrawny and discoloured by the dust. Most of them lie sprawling on the over-heated ground, motionless as small piles of trash left out for the dustman. The other canine creatures, just as incapable of motion, manage miraculously to stand on their legs. Even erect, you get the impression they're lying down fast asleep. Compared to my mother's frisky dog (a feisty creature so given to dribbling that it quivers and dribbles in its sleep), it feels like I'm dealing with a totally different species more related to the sloth stuck to its branch. Referring to them as "strays" seems as inappropriate as the idea of a wandering tree or a galloping plant.

Usually, I'm not excessively fond of animals. My zest for dogs remains very limited: that combination of dribble, fleas and bites leaves me little inclined to seek out their company. But I am here to astonish myself. I therefore stop in front of one of these fleabags (probably also afflicted with a number of incurable diseases) and surprise myself by caressing the bony body of a Siamese canine (with my bare hand).

As for the canid in question, it scarcely seems surprised by my gesture, despite the fact that it mustn't witness it on a daily basis. It stays there impassively, a dandy of the sewers. My caress (though meritorious given the fetid odour it emits) doesn't seem to give it any more pleasure than I get. My self-civilizing mission would have me kiss it on the nose or rummage up its anus with my tongue but I haven't yet reached that level of abnegation.

After having stroked another shabby ear as

I go by, I head for the lapping sounds of the
canals. I am immediately hailed by a boatman
who offers me a canoe for the day. I take up
his offer despite my fear of giving myself over
to the unrelenting movement of the water, and
find myself in the middle of a most unstable
drunken boat. My queasiness returns immediately but I hold it off as best I can.

Before we reach the main market, we come
across a pirogue full of men with bald pates
and shaved off eyebrows. They are all dressed
identically in bright orange togas. It must be
a cargo of priests. The pirogue passes like a
floating orangery.

Other fruits follow, piled up in mounds,
one fruit packed against the other, fruit whose
form and texture I find most intriguing: the
pirogue looks like a fruit store from another
planet. Venusian drupes, round and smooth
and mellow; rather martial-looking fruit with
spikes and rough, belligerent-looking edges;
Jupiter-like fruit, sleek, phallic and rubbery;
sombre, earthy, Plutonian citrus fruit. And
finally, a whole series of Saturnine fruit that
look at you with a hairy, anthropophagous eye.

One of them in particular captures my
attention. I decide to acquire it on the spot.
A rough-edged colossus that looks as if it
weighs around five kilos. It's all spiked with
pyramid-like tips that no doubt leave the blades
of knives chipped. It's a real carapace turned

in upon itself and has the appearance of a huge armoured egg, something of a dinosaur ball, an abrasive-looking cannonball. I lay it down at the bottom of the boat to display it as a trophy in my room at the hotel.

In a bend of the canal, my guide stops next to a pirogue that's been unloaded of its fruit. It seems empty at first glance, but at the bottom of the boat lies a clutch of writhing snakes. With an expert hand, the boatman picks out a little snake from the mass and makes the gesture of putting it around my neck. Extremely reluctant, I nevertheless agree to have the poisonous offering placed around my nape and shoulders.

My eyes must contract to pin pricks when the reptilian garland wraps itself around me as the boatman attempts to reassure me by asserting that it's nothing but a "boa-boa", which I imagine means that it can only kill me by strangulation.

After a few minutes, though, I get used to the writhing touch of the scales, even managing to experience an almost pleasant sensation. I don't really feel like it, but to surprise myself I decide to purchase the giant worm as a travelling companion. The snake dealer asks me in gestural English if I want it living, dead or chopped to bits. I answer that I would like to keep it in one single piece for the moment.

The rest of the visit ends in silence. The presence of the little snake stops me from appreciating the fruit arrays and the smiles of the floating sellers. At one point, the little snake decides to slither in between the buttons of my shirt, making me feel the flicker of its tongue against my stomach, the unnerving undulation of its skin against my own. It's definitely astonishing: a bolt of lightning in the blood.

When evening falls, I return to the hotel in a trance, my body barely mine anymore. I have so many goose bumps I'm afraid the little snake will think I'm some kind of chicken recipe. In fact, I ask myself with a jolt of terror what I'm supposed to feed the snake so I don't wake up in the morning with my whole arm stuffed in its mouth.

As soon as I arrive at the hotel, I make it clear to the receptionist that I'm in urgent need of serpent food. He promptly has two half-crushed sparrows in a tiny, quivering cage delivered to my room. The barred box deposited in my hand is nothing but wing beats and smothered chirps: a kind of living sandwich. The very idea of opening the cage and letting the snake devour the birds suddenly makes me seasick.

Back in my room, the only thing I can think of is casting them all out the window, both serpent and birds. For someone who isn't particularly fond of animals, I've ended up with three of them in the same room. Waiting to see how I'm going to get myself out of this scrape, I put the small snake and the dinosaur fruit on a chair and place the miserable fledglings on a table at the other side of the room. Lying down on the bed, I feel like a human sacrifice laid out between bird and reptile.

But before I can come to a resolution, the living scarf unrolls itself from the chair, glides to the ground and heads for the table where its sandwich of crushed nestlings awaits. To my horror, it winds itself around the sparrow box and tries to crack it like a nut. The cage disappears in the serpent's embrace. A few seconds later, the chirrups become more muted and die out. The little snake uncoils to reveal the suffocated birds. I open the cage and let the contents fall onto the table. The reptile swallows them before me.

XIX

When I awaken, the snake seems to have vanished into my dreams. I have a feeling of intense relief until I discover it coiled around the water bucket in the bathroom, just as I was beginning to look forward to washing. My attempts to undo the Gordian knot it forms around the bucket are futile as the little snake is holding on tightly in its sleep.

I am thus forced to go back to bed, my skin sticky with the sweat of dreams and tropical heat. The night has been most tyrannical. Not a breath of air, even with the window wide open.

I no longer know what to do: remain in Bangkok or leave on the spot. The lack of oxygen is hardly conducive to rapid decision-making. The hours here all bake in the oven, one after the other, fried and then candied. You swallow them without taste, without really realizing.

I really only have one single obligation and that is to find Jean's opium provider and purchase three kilos of pipe powder and the poppy heads. The operation, I'm told, involves no risk. The consumption of opium is a national pastime in these parts and French customs turn a blind eye when it comes to the smoking of opium. According to Jean, the dealers in Bangkok and Chiang Mai will charge too much. He prefers me to go and seek out the *papaver somniferum* in the mountain tribes in the west of Siam. He claims a little mountain-climbing can't do me any harm. The worst thing in this affair is he says he has forgotten the name of the tribe in which the famous dealer I'm supposed to get in touch with is based. He can't even remember the dealer's name. In fact, I wonder if he hasn't deliberately forgotten so I surpass myself, so my Way of Sorrows is made harder still.

According to his patchy memories, the tribe in question could be called Lisu, Lahu or Lao, in any case a name beginning with L (or might it be the Karen, all things considered). Anyway, he leaves me well informed. Thankfully, I'm in no hurry. I have enough money to last more than six months here. Jean has added that he doesn't urgently need the opium either as he still has a stash in one of his drawers and another behind the radiator in the bathroom.

Overwhelmed by apathy, I'm unable to make the decision to leave today. Taking a shower seems like a sufficient decision to occupy the day. I wait for my snake to wake and gracefully vacate its place so that I can pour a bucket of

water over my head. In the meantime, I should
find a name for my companion, to encourage
ties of affection between the animal kingdom
and me. I could call him Mr. Mortal.

I call out to Mortal where he lies, coiled
up in the shower room, but my call remains
unanswered so I conclude that another name
has to be found. On impulse, I shout out "Jean!"
in a voice that's louder than I intended and (oh
joy) the snake uncoils and comes to join me on
the bed. I'm astounded that Jean is proving to
be so receptive and obedient.

Wandering around the neighbourhood, I
come across a cluster of leggy huts perched like
skeletal spiders on top of stilts. Those hovels
have neither doors nor windows and you can
see a good deal of what they contain, from the
"bathroom" (a bucket of water) to the parental
suite (a bed of hemp on the bare ground). In
the open doorways, the children, naked to the
age of puberty, are busy playing marbles. A
parental foot sticks out of an opening and seems
to censor misbehaviour from time to time. A
hammock sways in the background, weighted
with sleeping ballast.

A little liquid fruit now bursts on my fringe,
trickling down my forehead. I instantly fear a
bird dropping, but it is only water. The first
drop of rain in the season, if the reactions
around me are anything to go by.

When the dark stains start falling to the
ground, a bevy of children bursts out of their
hives to swallow the honey of the rain. They
give themselves over to pleasures that I would
never have considered: to let your tongue tingle
with rain, to receive the slap of a drop in the
palm of your hand, to feel the big marbles of
rain slap and pool at the back of your throat,
to gag a little when the drop hits its target and
roar with laughter.

For raindrops in this place are very different
to the tight droplets that fall over Europe;
in Indochina, drops have corpulence. They
don't fall thick and fast—so each drop has
elbowroom. It slaps the ground with gluttony
and spreads its grease like an oil stain.

I give myself over to this shower of big
pooling rain flakes. My clothes are soon laden
with warm water, my shoes stick to my feet
at every step, making loud suction noises and
mucky gurgles.

A flurry of torn umbrellas stops and starts
again around the hustle and bustle of the stalls.
I buy a shiny bunch of bananas, half a dozen
soggy biscuits and a kind of large, unidenti-
fiable fritter.

Laden with purchases, I try to go back to my
place. I take three wrong turnings and finally
manage to deposit the water-soaked sponge that
I have become in the lobby of the hotel. I trail

my clothes like the sodden shreds of a tarpaulin,
feeling like a giant snail.

As I pass, for the second time before I've
arrived, the beaming receptionist throws off the
words *woman she-she* in the interrogative mode.
With a comprehending smile, he gestures for
me to return to my room and dashes off into the
street in search of one of those skin goddesses.

Someone knocks on the door. Already. I
stand there, not knowing what to do, barely
daring to breathe, a smoking sock in my hand,
my clammy foot in the air. Without further ado,
I pull the wet sock back on my foot and thrust
my drenched foot into the spongy shoe.

I come to a halt again, my hand trembling
on the handle. I give the door a brisk tug.

The mousey harlot that presents herself
is slender, very young. She must be around
fourteen, at the most. Bewildered, I sputter and
point to the stairs with an over-hesitant finger.
My mouth opens and closes. But instead of
stepping back, the young hussy slips under my
arm and deposits her trickling umbrella in a
corner of the room.

Feebly, I protest, a little mesmerized by the
unembarrassed poise of this budding woman.
Striding resolutely towards me, she starts to
unbutton my shirt. When I lay a hand on the
next button to stop her, she withdraws my
fingers with a gesture of annoyance.

Within the space of a few minutes, I find myself naked, steaming and quivering. Without warning she starts to lick at my skin, lapping the rain off my body. The little wet flickers of her tongue feel like darts in my flesh. I notice that another part of my flesh is also starting to soar. At the height of my erection, the little Siamese woman moves away slowly to watch me shudder, pierced by my own genital stinger.

And then she kneels in front of me and slips her dark lips around my glans. She shoves the nail of my flesh into the opening in her face. An unbelievable gentleness fills me from cock to foot until I fall to the ground in a moment of faintness. My penis slides out of her mouth with the popping sound of a cork flying out of a bottle. I find myself on the ground looking at it quiver and buck like a fish out of water.

Without showing the slightest surprise, as if her customers had a habit of fainting several times a day, she lies down on my legs and continues to suckle harder than ever, triggering a spurting whimper in my throat. When the tide of pleasure slowly withdraws its foam, the young vamp moves back up to sit on my belly, holding her mouth out towards mine. Closing my eyes, I wait for her lips when a flow of warm albumen slithers onto my tongue and into my throat. I look at her wide-eyed, but she just smiles, encouraging me to drink the white liquid that's still spilling out of her purplish lips.

XX

Rid of the cumbersome linguistic apparatus that usually makes men feel compelled to talk, to fill silence like a shameful hole, we indulge in the pleasure of contemplation.

I move over to the reception desk and place my elbows on the teak counter, letting out a sigh of exhaustion and a burst of laughter. The man and I exchange a few jerks of our respective laughter-shaken shoulders.

He nevertheless decides to shift to verbal communication, asking me with much nodding if the "woman" was "nice-nice".

"Nice-nice-nice", I answer, equally seized by a frenzy of nodding.

"Woman you like?"

"Yes, yes, yes ..."

"More woman she-she?"

"More?"

"Other she?"

"Yes ..."

And then I come out with an ill-considered sentence that's both too long and idiomatic:

"Actually, I thought the lady you sent me was a bit on the young side. Would you mind finding a slightly older woman? I'm nineteen years old."

The spell is broken.

He gives me a wary stare, as if I have snubbed or excluded him deliberately.

A little shamefaced, I try to limit my thoughts to the bare minimum.

"Bigger woman." I raise my hand to indicate height and more advanced years.

"Big woman, you like?"

"Bigger, older ..."

"Biggeroler ..."

"No, *old*, you know ..." And to indicate age, I mime a hunched elderly woman, bent over her cane. But I realize immediately that that's a tactical error.

"You like???!"

"Not old ... Older."

"Older-older ... Now?"

"Well, how about this evening?"

"Even ing, ah yes. Even ing."

I'm determined to repeat the experience as quickly as possible. My body is now eaten away by desire for women. I want to see mountains of breasts and mounds of Venus's mons.

This time, the love merchant that presents herself on my doorstep looks over seventy-five.

I don't know what to do. The door is already open.

Disconcerted, I stand there before her. I cannot in all decency send her back.

She stares at me, looking almost hurt, anticipating rejection. I step back from the entrance, making a sign for her to come into the room. She drags her feet, almost limping. The pockmarked surface of her skin reminds me of a kind of overdue crème brûlée. A curtain of flaccid flesh hangs from her jawline. I'm not sure I want to see her naked.

But the moment she sits on the bed, the aged streetwalker starts to undress. Against all expectations, she uncovers a slightly sagging, but full bosom. In fact, her body seems to be a different age to her face, as if the two parts of her being have aged at different paces.

She beckons for me to approach, and as soon as I am within reach she begins without warning to nibble my fingers, my arms, my thighs, my penis through my pants. She pulls me abruptly and I fall headlong on top of her. With mounting frenzy, we bite each other's flesh, shoulders, arms, stomach, chest. Her skin has the very fine texture of millefeuille pastry.

There are moments when I have the strange sensation of biting my own grandmother (something I always wanted to do as a child when she pushed me away with her foot).

My erection droops a little as I have this sorry thought, but it picks up again better than ever when grandma licks her middle finger and

stuffs it up my anus to pull me towards her.
The nimble finger is well-timed and makes Jean
reappear inside me.

I end up having sandwich intercourse
between a millefeuille grandmother and
an invert ghost. The result is actually quite
persuasive as I suddenly hear grandma climax.
A young voice. There must be something about
coitus that makes you younger.

The next morning, I tell Preecha (the philanthropic receptionist's name) that Kus (the name
of the aged lady of the night) was a little too old
to my taste. He tells me with much nodding of
the head that he fully understands (which leaves
me a little worried about what comes next) and
that he will make up for his error that very
evening.

As I wait for the evening to come, I wander
about the streets of Big Bangkok, thinking of
Jean. Our ghostly coupling has revived my
feelings for him and I'm depressed once again at
the thought that he no longer wants me.

In one of the city centre markets, I let myself
be coaxed into buying a photograph of the king
of Siam dressed in full regalia. The zealous
huckster explains to me that the king is sacred
in this country and that his image will bring me
luck. Seeing that I don't take his image seriously
enough, he warns me immediately that anything
that might offend the dignity of the king is
punishable by hanging (he mimes the hanging

rope with his tongue sticking out). I answer that it's good to know that. I'll keep it in my pocket in case I feel like committing suicide. He fails to understand my rejoinder.

Going back to the hotel, I resolve to leave Bangkok soon for this sedentariness is starting to make me dwell on morbid thoughts.

My carnal discoveries are obsessing me so much I'm incapable of being satisfied with such brief encounters. I need another travelling companion, or I'll be too tempted to end it all.

The decision restores my courage for what's in store, giving more coherent meaning to my venereal activities. I'm going to offer the next hustler I'm taken with to leave with me, for a daily salary that is high for her and moderate for me.

In the days that follow, a multitude of temptresses of all ages passes before and against me. I find them all attractive and disarming and am at a loss as to which one to choose, until Preecha introduces me to two young bawds that fascinate me instantly because they are twins. Separately, they are perhaps nothing special but as soon as they are side by side, something supernatural occurs. To this strangeness is added the fact that they both have a strong squint, a peculiarity that gives their multidi-rectional gaze a kind of cubist charm, a sort of intoxicating multiplicity.

Despite the visual ubiquity of my two streetwalkers, I have difficulty considering them in the plural. For when the three of us are reunited, it feels as if there are in fact only two of us. They are so identical I struggle to tell them apart: even their beauty spots are in the same place. Their hair is the same length and they dress the same way. I'm also convinced that they sometimes swap clothes after intercourse, but I am unable to be certain of this.

Their names are very different, but names are useless to me, for when I utter one of them in the hope of telling them apart, if only for a few minutes, they both raise their head as if they also both have the same name.

Their understanding of English is limited, but it's sufficiently elaborate for us to exchange a little personal information, as well as the basics so that we can understand one another with regard to practical matters such as moving.

After a moment of hesitation, they exchange a glance and concede to follow me to Chiang Rai, in the north of Siam. We agree to leave the next morning, to take the Bangkok Express which goes, despite its name, at the cruising speed of twenty-three kilometres an hour.

Weighed down by my bags, the dinosaur fruit and Jean around my neck, I meet my Siamese wenches on the platform of the *sathaané rôt fai*, which means "train station" in Siamese. I quickly understand why they call it "satanic

rot" for when the train comes in, it pours blades
of rocky grating noises in my ears.

I am hardly delighted at the idea of
spending two days and a night at the heart of
this unending rot, but the other solution (a week
and a half on a donkey's back or an elephant's)
hardly enthuses me more.

Also coughing up black smoke, I hand their
tickets to the twins who hurry over to find our
seats aboard the sumptuous carriage. We are
seated in first class, but the difference between
first and third class in this train is difficult to
discern. It seems mostly to lie in the price of
the ticket. The chairs are certainly made out
of elephant leather, but the worn out look of
the seats suggests they have been assaulted by
a million bottoms, a thousand rough fruits, a
thousand rodents.

We finally arrive in front of the first
windows of our carriage, but our seats seem to
have long been occupied. All is luxury, calmness
and a willingness to sit on other people's seats.
I nevertheless manage to seat the two twins next
to a buxom market gardener.

Jiggled by the train, we leave the station,
accompanied by a pack of rail squeals and
burps. We are soon in the countryside. Bangkok
and its teakwood temples are dwindling in the
distance.

We also gather speed, going beyond the
speed of sound (for the screeching of the

wheels seems to reach us in a deferred way, as
if behind us). Insects rain in through the open
windows (to avoid suffocation of the passengers
in the fug). In my neck, in my hair and in my
eyes, I get a drizzle of crickets, of frenzied
midges, of grasshoppers, mosquitoes, greenish
insects, flies, earwigs, flying roaches.

Kafka

XXI

When I arrive, clouds of dragonflies are flitting about in every direction. Accompanying the train, they settle on every window. Iridescent shreds of vibrating rainbow. As many dragonflies as there are mosquitoes in Venice.

We get off at the last stop on the line, Chiang Mai, capital of dragonflies, after three days of screeching, blackish smoke and poor sleep.

The air teems and vibrates with Lilliputian biplanes. It's War of the Dragonflies. Looking at them, I feel myself floating in the skin of a *Luftmensch*, one of those air-borne vagabonds that levitate in the paintings of Marc Chagall.

Jean casts a greedy heavenward look (oh to swallow those bits of sky).

From here, we are to travel by elephant to Chiang Rai, and then take the boat to Tha Ton. The twin sisters call out; they've located the 11.30 pachyderm. We climb the steps up to the platform and settle as best we can on the grey lunar surface of the elephant's back.

Then everything is set in motion and the

bells start to ring. The terrestrial whale crushes the ground along with a certain number of nodding dragonflies. The twins take a real delight in contemplating the landscape. Jean tries unsuccessfully to strangle the elephant.

An hour later, our muscles are damaged forever (especially Jean who seems to have strained his neck). One of my testicles is missing. When the night finally falls, a few of the locals move around us, putting up tents, feeding the mastodons, dispersing mosquitoes thanks to a plume of green smoke that smells like dog wee.

Once the encampment is set up, the few travellers who have been following in our wake join us around the campfire. Our elephant taxi drivers start to grill diminutive creatures impaled on long skewers. The outline of the roasted animal suggests it's a toad, an intuition which our driver confirms, pointing a finger at the fire. He calls this traditional dish "deep frog".

A little queasy from excessive consumption of deep frog, we wake to the sound of elephants trumpeting.

The landscape soon undulates under our elephants. On each side of us lie the mirror-like lakes of the paddy fields. Seen from above, these fields are nothing but transparent glass reflecting the sky. The acidic leaves lurking under the paddy fields lie there, invisible.

From time to time, we pass a herd of houses, standing on their stilts like long-legged birds. Even far from the water, the habitations are all elevated, sometimes up to six feet above the ground. Is this intended to protect them from wild beasts or floods? Are they waiting for the deluge in their Noah's Arks?

When the city of Chiang Rai finally comes into sight, we crush the last glimmers of the dusk under the feet of our elephants. Every traveller is numb; each of us feels the cruel imprint of the elephant between our buttocks. So that we don't have to engage in any form of pedestrian self-transport—which would be undignified for a Westerner—the mahouts put us down at our respective hotels.

Slumped on the bed, I consider the twin sisters carefully undressing. Their clothes are always so neatly folded, carefully laid out in a square-shaped pile in the exact centre of the chair. Their gestures too are measured: when they settle down to straddle me or to be taken in another manner, it looks like they are unfolding and folding themselves onto me. Their undulations—even the vigorous ones—are always under control. Every millimetre of movement is calculated. There is never any skidding, never a single misstep.

And yet they reach their climax in different

ways. Neja—at least I think it's her—always lets
out a little timid yelp, whereas Anej is given
to noisy sobs, before resuming her calm and
regular breathing.

After coitus, we always untangle most
courteously, almost excusing ourselves, as in a
high-society evening, for an accidental knock:
I'm sorry for your pants, sir, no, no, it's my
fault, your shirt is all wet.

I cannot bear such distance in a relationship.
Even when we look each other in the eyes,
which rarely occurs because of their divergent
and convergent squinting, I see their pupils
contract. It's clear I'll never be more than
another John to them, perhaps a slightly
unusual customer, but a renter of flesh nevertheless for whom they carry out their duty in
due form. Their detached stares rebuff me like
a piercing needle. I will have to get rid of them.
Soon. As soon as I can.

XXII

We are taking a stroll in the town-centre bazar when I hear a voice from behind me:

"Mister Butterfly, Mister Butterfly!"

Before realizing that I am the one being designated thus, I instantly translate into French. Monsieur Papillon is being called. I am struck with stupor. Terrified, I freeze on the spot. Cocteau. It's Jean. No one else calls me that. I turn around and find myself face to face with a tout.

"Mister, butterfly. You want? Where you come from-from?"

Politely, he hands me a glass box that contains a frumpy-looking butterfly pinned to a piece of faded cardboard.

"Mister, butterfly. Is good butterfly. You like, you want? You take-take?"

My terror abates, giving way to deep disappointment. An hour later, I'm back to missing Jean terribly. I feel far from everything. Far from him, from myself, far from the twins, far, far, far away.

Lord Byron used to say that love is incapable of resisting seasickness. I thought I had drowned the intensity of my feeling for Jean in the Indian Ocean, but it's back again, rising up from the water, dripping like Venus's renascent body.

The double being Anej-Neja asks me if all is well. I answer that everything's fine and then start to tell her about my feeling of disarray, after which I change my mind, not being able to pronounce, never mind explain the word love, the word invert. Her eyes roll around in every direction. She nods several times, understanding that I do not wish to speak about it. I will never know what she thinks of me. I can no longer stand being in their company. I have to be alone. I must get rid of her as soon as the sun sets. If I can't do it in the evening, I'll get rid of her during the night.

I've been waiting hours for the twins to fall asleep. Their eyelids are like scales: when one of the women closes her eyes under the weight of drowsiness, the other one's eyes lighten and open. More than ever before, I have the impression that they are in fact one single person divided in two.

At long last, the four eyes of the two-headed twin close at the same time. I avail of the opportunity to gather my belongings and attempt to extract Jean who, of course, has gone and wrapped himself around my pillow.

Burdened by my bag, by Jean around my neck, by the dinosaur fruit strapped to my belt like a convict's ball, I let the door squeak a little, cast a last glance at the Twin as I seal off the door's complaint. Why bother leave a valedictory letter? All she needs is the money I have left her on the little bedside table to be free for a while.

Outside, the night is a dark grey. The moon is as veiled as the sun is diluted during the day by the fuzzy clouds of the tropics. Small islands of trash piled in the middle of the street turn out to be recumbent paupers, lying entangled. Clusters of people, dark and dirty, but warm and connected.

A skeletal cat buries its nose in the remains of a rat. A long cockroach bars my path, peers at me with undisguised greed lurking in its eyes. It's the size of Gregor Samsa, Kafka's cockroach. It seems famished. As I edge sideways to avoid it, it scuttles into my path again and will not let me pass. I try to outrun it, but nothing avails. It's hot on my heels.

Having finally outpaced it after a long chase through the streets of Chiang Rai, I stop before a street seller of litchis in the midst of his nocturnal nap (I say 'nap' because the notion of a full night's sleep doesn't seem to obtain in these parts—people sleep sporadically during

the day, from time to time during the night).
Without really waking up, the street vendor
proffers his litchis in a bowl of ingeniously-in-
terwoven leaves. Still asleep, he hands me my
change and lies back down without having
spared me as much as a glance. If he's in the
middle of a dream, it's definitely not one about
pilfering.

A few yards down the road, I come across
a cart whose front is lined with a curtain of
gangrenous sausages swaying in the breeze like
hangman's rope, each one blacker and more
worm-eaten than the next.

The night and the duty I have to astonish
myself get the upper hand, prompting me to
buy two sticks of gangrene. Darkness makes you
less cautious. It's the end of the day, the end of
a little life of twelve hours; you tell yourself that
dying at night is almost a natural thing.

The poison is dark as the night, the sausage
hard as an edible dagger. I sink my teeth
voraciously into mine. It has the tang of a
deadly disease.

My mouth smells like a self-neglecting
sausage. My heart is heavy; my stomach is sick.
I no longer know where I am going. Jean has
probably forgotten me and Tiresias is no doubt
going about his numerous occupations. My
mother is taking care of her dog. The frozen
photograph of my father on her bedside table
and the doggy-dog are enough for her. The

dog is there, leaving no room in her mind for a desperate son. And yet, I feel mothersick, and suffer like a dog.

I find myself on the outskirts of the city. Looming up above in the distance, I make out the indistinct outlines of the northern mountains. It is towards these that I am to direct my steps.

Behind me, I hear a small, rapid patter. I turn around to find Gregor Samsa hot in pursuit, dashing towards me with all his antennae deployed. I haven't given him the slip at all. He has tailed me, following in my tracks like a dog.

I run a little to tire him out, but Gregor is still there, hungry as ever. As he trots down the road towards me, his feelers wiggling like a Cerberus with many tails. I lift my foot. Gregor senses the smell of fresh flesh coming up close. He arrives at a gallop .... Squasssh! Mashed Gregor under my shoe. Mashed Gregor rubbed off on the footpath. And despite all that, the feelers keep nervously twitching.

I kneel in front of the remains on the edge of the pavement and with a vengeful finger disembowel the creature and bring its entrails to my lips. The taste of this filthy dreck is acrid, infernal. It's like a concentrated piece of filthy trash. But I am filled with the satisfaction of having accomplished yet another ordeal.

I cut into the rough rind of a litchi with
my teeth to get rid of the taste of putrefaction,
revealing the white flesh of the fruit. And just as
I am pausing to contemplate this comestible my
revenge plot comes to light.

The bared stone in the fruit resembles an
iris: Jean's eye.

Kokto

XXIII

Not having discovered a sense of supreme
wonder for Cocteau or myself, I will stick
to finding the opium dealer he is vaguely
acquainted with in the vicinity. All I have are
the names of a few tribes he has randomly cast
up in the air: Yao, Miao, Akha, Lao, Lahu, Lisu,
Karen.

An impossible quest launched by a cruel
child.

White pebbles lost in the ocean of a forest.

In the event, the first people I encounter
belong to the Lao tribe (I think, as I have the
greatest difficulty making myself understood,
even with gestures I thought were universally
understood by all of mankind).

When I arrive in the first ethnic village, I am
greeted by trees decorated with what looks like
hundreds of hangman's ropes.

I later learn that far from symbolizing
off-putting threats for intruders, these ropes are
actually the dried and hardened umbilical cords
of every member of the tribe. They can thus

go and consult this cord at every stage of their lives. The serpent of flesh that ties each being to his mother, to his origins like a Siamese twin.

I glide from village to village, looking for Jean but the Lao and the Yao seem to know neither Cocteau nor opium. I start to wonder if there are any opiates in Siam at all. When I ask if people know Cocteau, they invariably deform and echo my words in the local accent: "Kokto?", "Koktou?", "Kogta?" and even once "Bangkok?"

Finally, I am overjoyed to discover that the villages in the extreme north-west are great consumers of opium. The hills in this region are covered in poppies: whole fields of opiate bells caressed by flights of dragonflies.

At the other end of these hallucinogenic meadows, I spot a group of moving figures. The opium gatherers. They lift their heads to look at me: bare-breasted, their teeth blackened by betel juice, a long white pipe stuck behind their ears. They hold the key to Jean's heart in their hands. Not having found his regular supplier, I purchase a few high-priced poppy heads and the kilos of opium.

Big and heavy as a small tree trunk, Jean has now almost reached his adult size. It will be impossible to conceal him when I go through French customs. I must resolve to leave him in

Siam. I assess the possible solutions: putting
him back into his natural habitat, selling him,
eating him, starving him so he will eat me.

The last solution imposes itself as the most
logical of these. I still think about committing
suicide, but passively, spinelessly, the way you
think about something you should do, a sort of
necessary chore. My existence is a little like the
dirty tiling that should be scrubbed but remains
uncleaned, out of pure negligence. It's not as if I
am committing suicide out of idleness—rather, I
am like the allegory of laziness in Dante, so lazy
I can't even make myself crawl into purgatory.

There's another thing that bothers me in the
idea of suicide: it's the complete lack of surprise
it involves. Committing the act means having
to plan ahead, it means knowing the end of the
novel in advance, it means dying the way you
have lived, in the boredom of the habitual. If life
is a long-winded story that you tell yourself, let
it at least end with some surprise. Let it end it
on a striking scene, an unexpected twist.

But I'm sick of waiting for death to surprise
me. It's taking too long. I rush off the road
and plunge into the Siamese underbrush. The
vegetation is so dense it feels like I'm making
my way through a jungle of green spider web.
Vegetal luxuriance reaches such a degree of
intensity in this place it's as if there are two
superposed jungles: trees growing on top of
each other, plants stepping over plants. The

weeds run so wild here it looks like they're
scampering off in every direction, over tree
trunks and rocks; they pitch themselves up
into the air like hairdos, dishevelled in places,
plaited in others.

And then, contrary to all expectations, a
clearing. An opening of several metres where
you catch a glimpse of sky. A dim light drips
down the leaves. I put Jean down on a large slab
of stone next to the dinosaur fruit. I lie down on
the grass next to the stone and tie Jean's head
with one end of the loosened strap of my bag. I
tie the other end around my neck so that neither
of us is able to leave.

We watch the sky slowly flicker out.
Darkness is as nebulous here as the light. You'd
think the sky is never entirely clear. A blurry
moon begins to melt its hazy gleam.

Night favours reflection. You act by day; you
think at night. The light of day only sets the
scene for objects; darkness brings out matters of
the mind. Night makes life appear as it really is:
empty, weak, doomed to failure.

In those moments of nocturnal nihilism,
all you need is for a loved one to pass before
you, movingly delicate and beautiful, tottering
slightly in his sleep, his eyelids half-closed,
to prove that the exact opposite is true. But
when your beloved is no longer by your side,
the night proves to be without mercy, as
overbearing as death.

The day lights up again, and is extinguished once more. Jean is increasingly restless. He tugs like a battling demon at the strap around my neck. Sooner or later, he'll get too hungry and will decide to suffocate his master. I no longer eat, but hunger doesn't torment me for all that. I've lost my taste for the fruits of this earth. My heart skips and hops in its cage like an exhausted bat.

When I finally manage to fall asleep, I get bogged down in a recurring dream. Inexplicably, I find myself on a clifftop. Black night tormented by wind. Only the sound of the wind and the waves reaches my ears. A smell of burnt flesh seems to waft up from the land. I walk on the edge of the cliff on something like charred soil. It crunches and crackles like a bed of toast under my feet.

In the distance, I catch a glimpse of a figure that seems to be another human being.

I move prudently towards him. He edges towards me, his gait all out of kilter, his feet twisted in every direction. I come to a halt, a few steps away from him to ask him where we are, but he continues walking straight at me, his eyes sinister, malevolent.

It always begins in the same manner. Before I can open my mouth to utter a word, his arm shoots out to seize me by the throat.

The moment I sense his grip, I instantly know who he is.

I have had this dream many times. The man grasping me by the throat like a boa constrictor is Thanatos, my old enemy. The god of death. A sinister, lopsided shorty with a worm-eaten nose. His eyes crusty with crud at the edges. His irises are tawny, mud-coloured; his gaze both demented and depressed. His livid skin, his slick, dark hair neatly combed to the side. His upper lip sports a mean little moustache no larger than the bristle on the toothbrush I use to take the muck off my brown pair of boots to give them a shine. His teeth are yellow with decay. The smell escaping from his slightly open mouth is enough to make a jackal turn pale.

With slow gestures, taking his time, he crushes me with unbelievable savagery, lifting me clean off the ground with a single lifted arm, as if he is just saluting the crowd. I hang there at the end of his arm, unable to breathe.

And then, the same thing each time, he starts pulling out my teeth, one by one, tugging them out with the thumb and index finger of his right hand, casting them all into the void. Once my gums have been weeded and my mouth is left bloody and empty, he lowers his hand to my underbelly and takes hold of my testicles. He starts to strengthen his grip on my scrotum to crush it to a pulp, signalling his victory over Eros.

I hit his arms with all my strength. I slap him and tear at him with my nails, feebly spitting my blood in his face. All I manage to do is to speckle his cheeks and his mouth with tiny red dots. I kick him in his knock-knees. I battle like a demon, but nothing avails. My limbs are all flaccid; the strength emanating from his arms is by contrast infinite and implacable. His fist is a nub of gravity absorbing all the elemental force around us.

The dream always ends in the same way.

Just as I am about to succumb, he unexpectedly releases me. I fall, coughing my lungs out onto the calcined ground, my head toothless, my testicles crushed to a paste.

That's when he orders me to throw myself from the cliff.

I get up as best I can.

I dither for a moment at the top of the cliff.

And then I lift my foot and carry out the order, to release myself from his unbearable presence.

The drop is endless. I fall in slow motion. I feel the wind whistling against my face, the tang of the waves fills my nostrils, seagulls screech and squawk all around me.

I manage to pull myself out of this nightmare just before my skull smashes against the rocks. When I come to, my pillow covered in saliva, I still feel possessed. I have only one thought in mind, to put an end to it all.

XXIV

I didn't want to eat anymore; my body
decided otherwise. After eight days of fasting,
Jean was no longer moving. (Did he abstain out
of loyalty or because I was too big to swallow? I
will never know for sure.)

My trembling hands took hold of his body.
In truth, I did not know if he was still alive. He
was no longer moving, in any case. He failed
to react when I cut into him to lop a piece of
his tail off with my knife, as a keepsake. I was
so hungry I gnawed at it and kept the tip as an
offering for Kokto.

A little later, reinvigorated and restored, I
hoisted Jean's mutilated corpse onto the branch
of a tree and left him there in that godforsaken
clearing where no one will ever come, possibly
for centuries. I left him oscillating gently in the
wind like a rope, like an umbilical cord.

The squalor of Bangkok sprawls at my
feet again. This quarter of the city is more
like a pile of human detritus than a suburb:
you see wretches dragging their misshapen

bodies through the mud, their bones twisted
by polio. No doubt ravaged by leprosy, others
have missing fingers. I have my skin handled
on several occasions by a group of mutilated
mendicants.

After these trying experiences, I take refuge
in a Buddhist temple to collect my thoughts
and lay down the bag containing the dinosaur
fruit and the opium. I'm so spent, it feels like
the fruit has put on extra weight. I still can't
understand why I keep shouldering the burden.
I must think I'm Sisyphus.

In the middle of the temple, a few
orange-clad monks bow down before lotus
flowers. The feet of the Buddha are laden with
offerings of every kind: banknotes so wrinkled
with dirt they are no longer recognizable,
fossilized pastry, bits of golden paper, incense
sticks giving off a heady smell of lotus blossom.

I have to decide what I'm going to do here,
before I leave.

Burdening myself anew with my bags, I take
refuge in a darkened corner of the ambulatory,
but there is nothing to discover here, no niche
or crypt. It's all there in the centre: a single
gigantic, golden Buddha. There is nothing
to hide in this religion, no mystification, no
Judas-like bribe, just the brightness of the
Buddha. Religious mysticism available to all and
sundry.

Moving forward into the ambulatory, I come

across a teakwood table where a monk's gown lies in state, carefully folded into the shape of a lozenge. I lay my hand on the orange textile, stroking the preternaturally watered fabric. It feels like I'm caressing the silken skin of God. Every particle in my being suddenly feels a deep craving to make this skin my own. I must have it.

I will be turned into an orange monk. Something with which to surprise Jean before he receives his final astonishment.

To avoid arousing suspicion, I take another discreet walk around the temple, and as soon as the three monks are out of sight, I purloin the gown, stuffing it as quickly as I can into one of my bags. I exit the temple, a drum beating in my chest. I don't know the punishment meted out for theft in this country, but I know that in this part of the world one can be chastised by having one's hand cut off.

The ferry leaves for Marseille in a few hours and I wish to end my life again. I walk round in circles on the quay. The wind scatters the gulls.

I have my cyanide pill left: the little photo-graph of the Siamese king. All I have to do is take it out in front of someone—anyone at all, even a child—and stamp on it or tear it to shreds and that will do the trick, I'll be carried off to prison. I'll be euthanized without having to worry over the details, the chore of having to deliver the death blow. All I have to do is switch on the machine and the rest will unfold beyond my will. I'll be taken away like a bag of potatoes in a freight car. I will be taken care of like a child. I will have nothing to do.

I take the photograph out of my jacket. The king is there, standing to attention, with knotted tie, decked out in medals. I take my pen and start to doodle a Salvador Dali-like moustache on his face. I add a smoking dog turd to his brow, a few strategically-placed carbuncles, shaggy nasal hairs, an enormous pair of spectacles—

"Sir?"

With a spasmodic gesture, I stuff the pen and the photo deep into the bag.

"You're drawing?"

"No. I'm … not drawing. I'm … taking notes."

"You write?"

"… yes."

"Can I ask what you're writing?"

"Yes, I … I'm writing a kind of … novel."

"A novel?"

"To tell you the truth, it's more of a diary than anything else, for the moment."

"My lover is also writing one. I haven't read it yet."

"Has he finished it?"

"I don't really know. We don't see each other anymore."

"You've fallen out?"

"We love each other bitterly."

"Bitterly?"

"We're separated."

"And why is that?"

"My father doesn't love me."

"I must admit I don't quite follow the logic of what you're telling me, Mademoiselle."

"Otherwise, he wouldn't oppose our union."

"So why is he opposing your union?"

"Because the age gap between us is too wide and because I haven't come of age yet."

"I'm not twenty-one either."

"Eighteen, you mean. No. On top of that, my lover was ... he was my former French teacher. Which is why I wanted to ask you if you were taking the boat later on."

"Well ... I do have a ticket. I'm scheduled for departure."

"Are you going back to Marseille?"

"Yes. Well, Paris, actually. But the boat stops in Marseille, of course."

There's something in her eyes. Something which almost escapes comprehension. She reminds me of a brown-haired Camille Aude.

"Would you very much mind putting this envelope in a letterbox when you arrive? Preferably in Marseille. My lover lives in Aix-en-Provence."

"Of course. I'll take care of it."

"You're so kind. Letters sent from here

rarely reach their destination. They get lost on the way, or someone takes the stamps and sells them. People here are so poor."

"I understand."

I see what it is now. There's a kind of flower in her eye. Her iris is green, but in the middle, just around the pupil, yellow sparks glow. Like petals of fire. It feels like I'm looking down at a sunflower from above, a sunflower lying on a bed of green grass.

"Thanks again, Sir. You look kind, just a little bit tired. You should take a rest. Anyway, have a safe journey. And enjoy that drawing of yours!"

She lets out a laugh and leaves. A flowery wink. Her laughter, fresh, tender, light-hearted. She turns around one last time. I palpate Cocteau's opium bulbs in the bag. A blithe hand reaches upward, caresses the air and falls back. Her shape dwindles and she stops turning around. She disappears into the crowd. All that remains of her is the curly French writing on the envelope. I have been entrusted with yet another important task.

The liner's portholes shiver in unison. The wash stirred up by the engines raise goose bumps on the waves. The mooring ropes are almost all untied. We are bound to dry land by only a thread or two. Here I go again, off for a month of quicksand in the guts.

They say that seasickness is mostly in the head. If you concentrate hard enough, you're supposed to be able to avoid regurgitation. A little autosuggestion is supposed to do the trick. Thomas, you will not vomit. Thomas. You will not vomit.

Thomas vomits abundantly. It only works in theory, like the remedy for shyness.

I head for the reception desk which is giving newspapers away for free. I leave carrying off *The Bangkok Times*. On the front page, it says *"Homosexuals Join Jews in Camps"*. I manage to read a few lines about the phenomenon described. I discover that inverts in Germany are now expected to wear a pink triangle. There's also a rumour that in the detention centres for illegals, soldiers use the pink triangles stitched to the prisoners' chests for target practice. It's said that homosexuals have their testicles melted down with boiling water.

I reread these lines and am suddenly taken with a strong urge to vomit again. A yellowish jet shoots out of my mouth, splattering the newspaper. Shaken by a fit, I fail to fold it in time to hold back the mess.

My vomit trickles heavily onto the carpet in front of the reception. A string of saliva is still leaking out of the open mouth of the newspaper. I fold and refold it as best I can, enveloping the slimy matter into a hard ball of paper.

Brow-beating stares. Grimaces of disgust.
Loud voices invoke decorum.

I beg your pardon. So sorry.

If the Evening Is Impossible

XXV

After a week of seasickness, during which
I vomit my guts out as well as all my recent
memories, the ship's physician declares that
the frequency of my vomiting is abnormal.
The waxy aspect of my eyeballs has made him
come to the conclusion that I may be suffering
from jaundice. He even admits that he should
no longer be in contact with me as what I am
afflicted with is in all likelihood contagious.

I am to avoid all contact with others, he
adds. I must touch no one on the skin and even
refrain from breathing too close to anyone.
He thinks I may have contracted a rare and
dangerous form of the disease. I can either die
of it or recover without aftereffects. When he
learns that I have allowed myself to be touched
by lepers, that I have eaten both a cockroach
and rotting meat, his eyes open wide and he
gives me a right telling off ("you are completely
reckless, young man").

He is mistaken: I am well aware of what I
am doing. There will be no missing this time. I

will hit all my targets, Cocteau included.

During the crossing, despite the queasiness,
I grow accustomed to the sea, my health begins
to stabilise. None of my fingers has fallen off,
for the time being. My stool remains yellow
and my urine is brown (I find myself smitten
with corporal astonishment) but my vomiting is
reduced to one or two belches for breakfast and
a mouthful of vomit for my four o'clock snack.
Otherwise, despite the retching, it's *vade retro
vomitas*.

A week before our arrival, I decide to turn
myself into an orange monk to get used to the
gown before appearing in front of Cocteau. A
full dress rehearsal in stage costume.

Facing the mirror in my cabin, I shave off
my hair and my eyebrows, in keeping with
Siamese monastic customs. Once the task is
accomplished, I have trouble recognizing myself
in the mirror. A yellowish face topped with a
skullcap of pasty albumin-like flesh. By contrast,
as I have both tanned and yellowed, the conti-
nuity between my skin and the orange toga is
almost perfect.

While in France, yellow is traditionally the
colour of cuckolds, in India it is the colour of
pariahs. In this twofold attire, I am thus both a
pariah and a cuckold.

When I lounge around the upper decks
of the ship, I get brow-beaten by the other

passengers, as if my disguise was in terribly
poor taste (which is no doubt true). I am given
to understand it is improper to strut around
in such garb, being but a few kilometres from
European coastlines. Shaven monks are all well
and good in Siam, but quite another kettle of
fish within a stone's throw of France. Out of the
corner of my eye, I spot the Mortels, the Ladies
of Veauregard, full of indignation at my lack of
breeding. When I sit in the restaurant, people
clear the floor as if I had just established the
Salpêtrière hospital at their table. I turn on them
my cold, diseased disdain.

But my disdain lifts with the jabber of
Marseille's sea gulls. July's sun is quivering
like a fried egg in the sky. The steep rocky
coasts of the azure creek are already nibbling at
the horizon. The liner shakes itself. Umbilical
cords are unleashed and tied once again to the
bollards of the fatherland. The mooring lines
tauten. Passengers are requested to disembark.

I'm in the Train Bleu, the navy blue train
that shuttles between the capital and the
southern sea. After months of absence, France
has become as alien to me as Siam was before I
arrived in Indochina.

A man wearing a cap comes in to check our
tickets. He leaves a little hole in each ticket. The
Paris-Lyon-Mediterranean wishes you a pleasant
journey.

In a few hours, I will find myself in front of one of the country's greatest writers once again. What will I tell him? Or rather, what will I do to him? I will find myself before him, a flocculent ghost, a revenant back from the dead to haunt him, to kill him, when the necessity arises.

Can one really claim to love a person one is ready to stab? Probably not. If I don't kill him out of love, I will kill him out of despair, because there is nothing else to do. He no longer wishes to be with me. I do not know where to go. What is one to do with an empty shell of a life? There's the motive: emptiness.

All I have to do now is find the murder weapon. I no longer have enough money to purchase a revolver. This will therefore have to be a poor man's crime. Knives can be obtained at a reasonable price. Cheaper still: defenestration. I push him out with a big friendly slap on the back. Better still: I throw myself out into the air with him, since it is out of vacuity that I am killing him. The call of the void, the whistling of the air in our ears, followed by the impact cementing the void forevermore.

Or else, I can avail of his cane-sword, always lying in the same spot, to the right of the door. But I have tried that before. Too bloody. It requires too much courage. I need something easier.

But I already have an idea in mind. I thought of it with Gregor. I will administer death with a mere kiss. Cocteau's health is poor, he can only succumb to the highly communicable disease I carry within me like a dagger. I am myself a potent poison—a serpent in the guise of a friend, disguised as me, disguised as a monk, as a sickly monk driven by a dark force that I fail to understand.

The train reaches its raging speed, a mechanical lion roars against the rails. We are knocked about on our berths. A freight train. A train always brings its passengers to their implacable fates. It cannot take unexpected turns, alternative routes; everything is determined in advance.

XXVI

If the evening is impossible, phone. The handset receiver slips in my hand. Sweaty, sweaty. I can't stop perspiring. When I hear the operator's voice, I say "Gutenberg 29 41". She answers "please hold the call for a moment", but the wait is interminable.

He's not in. He has left, he's no longer in the same hotel.

But then, against all odds, I hear his throaty voice, thin as his hands. It's him. He's just up. It's still dark. I didn't think it was that early. Repeating himself, he says:

"Yes, this is Cocteau, listening ..."

"Jean ...?"

"Yes, who is this?"

"It's me."

"Can you speak up, please?"

"It's me!"

"Well, I know a lot of people called me around here."

"It's Thomas."

"Thomas ...? Why are you calling me at this unearthly hour? Where are you?"

"I'm back."

"Back? But I saw you yesterday."

"Yesterday? That's impossible. I wasn't here yesterday."

"Who are you, then?"

"It's Thomas Hearse."

"Ah, Hearse! So sorry, my boy. I didn't think I would see you so soon. So, how did your trip go? Did you find my favourite flower?"

"The opium is in the bag. Three kilos of poison. As promised. And a bagful of seed heads. Can I come and see you?"

"Now?"

"Yes."

"Alright, alright … Fine. I'll get myself prepared. I'll be waiting. Are you sure you're alright? You seem a bit peevish. Just tired, perhaps?"

"Yes, that's it. See you in a moment."

I'll pour the opium powder over his prostrate body the way people used to be buried in the sand along the coast.

The temple of the Madeleine is there before me. Saint Luke stands, as decapitated as ever. Nothing has changed because nothing can change.

Hello, Mr. Porter. Yes, I'm going up to Mr. Cocteau. Does that bother you?

The door stands before me, as daunting as the first day. I'm on the point of knocking when the phone rings inside. I feel like a character in a detective novel.

The ring tone ceases. I hear a muffled voice
answering. Someone hangs up. Then, a few
steps. A hand on the handle of the door. I feel
like fleeing. Too late.

He looks at me, a wary expression on his
face. He doesn't recognize me.

His cane-sword is in his hand. His neck is
devoured by hives.

"Thomas?! Is that you? ... My God ... You're
unrecognizable ... What's happened? Have you
shaved your hair? What were you trying to
achieve? Your eyebrows too ... It's impossible to
recognize you. What got into you? ... And that
gown. You look like a monk from Indochina."

"I did it to surprise you."

"Well, you've certainly achieved that ...
Come, do come in. I'm so sorry for giving you
such a poor welcome. The receptionist just
called to say that a crazy man in a gown was
trying to get into my room. Anyway, what a
fright for nothing. Ah, so! Let me introduce you
to Albert. My ... my friend. Albert is an actor.
I'm going to help him to make it in the world of
theatre."

It feels like the young man he's introducing
me to is me. He's my height and he has the
spontaneous gestures I used to have before I fell
ill. He must be my age and seems barely artic-
ulate. He has retreated into silence to preserve
his mystery. Like me when I first started, out of

fear of blurting out something asinine.

Seeing that I'm not moving towards him, he reaches out, a cryptic look on his face. If I take his hand, he will run the risk of contracting the terrible illness that's gnawing away at me.

Tough luck. He seems so intent on shaking my hand. Too much enthusiasm is bad for your health.

He's also handsome. As handsome as I am ordinary.

"What about Nathalie?"

"Nathalie ... She ... We've parted. She was unable to cope with what people were saying about me. My paramours, opium. She's gone back to the United States. Would you care for a cup of tea?"

"No, thanks, I ... won't be staying. I must ... Here, take the seed heads. And the opium powder. I wasn't able to find your supplier, but someone helped me out."

"Yes, I'm so sorry. I've felt so guilty about that. My contact here told me the dealer no longer lives in Siam. He currently takes care of a plantation in Burma. You know, those tribes don't really recognize the borders between countries: Siam, Burma. It's just one territory to them. But oh, how I felt bad about this. I wanted to go and fetch you in Indochina. And then Tiresias said it would be better for you to manage on your own. Rites of passage and so on. You know him ... Anyway, I'm happy to see you're in good ... Are you alright, at least? Are you in good health? You're a bit waxy-looking. You look exhausted. You have to rest, my boy. You might as well lie down on the bed for a few hours. Albert is going to make some tea and get us a little snack."

"No, really, I have to go. Thanks."

"Thomas ... Let me at least bring you back to your mother."

"No, I don't want to see her. And I have something to do."

"Can I ask what is taking you away from us so urgently after such a long voyage?"

"No. Farewell, Jean. Goodbye ... Albert."

At the door, he seizes me by the wrist. His hives are even eating his cheek. Immobilized by the contact of his fingers against my palm, I fail to stop him quickly enough from putting his hand on my skull in blessing. The hand is cool. A starfish on a rock. He gives me a kind, anxious stare. I feel like weeping, at last.

He closes his eyes and starts to move forward to put his thin-lipped mouth on mine.

"Move away from me."

"Please forgive me, Thomas ... I'm better at making friends than at making love. I've told you that before."

"It's already done. It's all forgiven. I came here with the intention of transmitting the disease I have in me. Seeing you so happy, I've been unable to go through with it ... And I've come to the realization that I mostly love you because I cannot love myself. You know, there are times when I imagine I'm you, that I draw the way you do, that I wrote *The Holy Terrors*, *The Infernal Machine*. You might say I become your character, Thomas the Imposter. And then the dream fades and I find myself in my own hellish skin again, stuck within the four walls of my poor head. I'll never be you. I don't have it in me. You're so brilliant you manage to make people forget you're not so handsome; I'm incapable of doing that. I have to accept that I'm mediocre on all levels. I think that after all that solitary suffering, I've developed murderous impulses towards you ... You would do well to get out of my way. I don't really know myself anymore. I'm not your Mr. Butterfly. I'm no longer Thomas. I'm only Hearse now."

The Second Eye

XXVII

My bag and coat are still lying where I left
them on the bridge. No passers-by at this hour.
The tramps are still asleep.

I pull my dinosaur fruit out of the bag
and hold it in my hands above the water. The
abrasive nubs on the surface of the fruit print
their triangular shapes into my palms. What
a strange piece of fruit. There's something
primordial and immutable about it. It has
neither matured nor changed its appearance
in the few weeks it has spent climbing and
descending the hills of Siam on my back. As
heavy as ever, as enigmatic as before.

Giving it no further thought, I pull my
hands apart and let the whole mass of its weight
plummet onto my splintered reflection. It
sinks like a cannon ball in a stream of bubbles.
I see it coming up on the other side of the
bridge, floating vaguely beneath the surface,
a miscarried foetus cast into the water by
murderous parents.

His car was low and streamlined. The long scarf
wrapped around his neck floated in the air and got
caught in the axle. It strangled, decapitated him
furiously, while the car skidded, mashing itself,
rearing up against a tree to become a ruin of silence
with a single hub spinning slower and slower in the
air like a lottery wheel.

Taking the gown off, I find myself bared.
Naked as Adam on Mirabeau Bridge. A slight
breeze caresses my skin. The morning sun melts
a few of its rays on my chest and my belly. I
start to twist the gown in on itself, twining it
stiffly until it's rigid as rope. I fasten it to a
lamppost, holding the other end between my
legs. I tie that end around my neck, just above
my Adam's apple. I am now graced with a long,
orange snake. Here I am, dressed for my last
trial by water. Thanatos has pushed me once
more to this extremity. I hear his command in
my ear.

I climb up on the metal railing, precariously
balanced. The Eiffel Tower has unveiled a little
of its spider web in the glimmer of the dawn.
I should reflect. Formulate a deep thought. Or
just a pretty turn of phrase. But I no longer
wish to think and am beginning to waver on the
railing. There's no point in thinking. It's all said
and done. I'm utterly valueless. Worth less than
nothing. A man without qualities, devoid of
interest, not worth considering, shunned by my

own ineptitude, beyond the pale of humanity. A useless dolt, I deserve only contempt. Paltry and pathetic. I couldn't even hold a candle to a *Luftmensch*. Chagall's vagabonds can at least float and hold themselves up in the air.

Jean often says that in his view existence is a horizontal fall. I'm going to try the vertical version of that. I'll be a perforated *Luftmensch*, passing from life viewed from above to life seen from below in a matter of seconds.

Bending my knees and hunkering down a little on the handrail, I cast myself into the void in the hope that it will be quick, that my neck will be snapped.

I've often asked myself what a hanged man feels when his neck fails to break, when he opens his eyes again after the violent tug of the rope.

The physiological phenomenon that provokes erections in the most impotent hanged men has been given much attention in writing, as if it was the equivalent of having a vagina around one's neck. Well, I can tell you, it's nothing like it. After the pain provoked by the backlash, the brutal jolt that you feel is like a near decapitation. At most, you feel a vague sensation of vertigo in your crotch, the kind of sensation you get in your loins when you're going too fast on a swing. Even my death will have lacked potency.

Spinning round on my axis at the end of this unwinding rope, I scarcely feel more hanged than usual. My throat is more tightly tied and painful, certainly. I'm a little redder and more strangled than when I encounter someone I'm drawn to.

It's getting harder and harder to breathe. I see myself dangling naked, slowly turning like a spinning top in the final rounds, as the coloured gown twists and untwists. I turn like a spider suspended at the end of its thread. A spider caught in its own trap.

I am still thinking these outlandish thoughts, right up to the moment I stop breathing entirely and things start to go awry. I suddenly feel small, the way I used to feel as a child putting my head under the thick hide of the blankets deep inside the bed. At first, I found it wonderful, uncharted, forbidden territory, an archaeological dig into the womb. After a few minutes, though, I would start to feel the lack of air and the unbearable difficulty of having to turn back in time and struggle out of sheets turned into straightjackets.

The gown is strangling me with its implacable arm. I pull myself up to relieve the suffocating grip of the fabric, but the knot remains tight, having gained a marble-strong hold on my neck. With a feverish trembling hand, still weakened by jaundice, I try to hold back the fabric a few brief instants so I have time to loosen up the gown's muscles; with my other hand, I try in vain to loosen the knot. It's hard as a stone; my muscles soft as slugs.

The pressure becomes terrible, unbearable.

I only manage to wedge the tip of my trembling forefinger into the hard nub of the knot. But then my survival instinct rises up in me like a wild animal. Lifting myself up weakly with both hands tugging on the gown, I start to bite into the fabric above the knot with bewildering rage. I bite into it so hard my teeth practically shatter. My mouth is full of blood. I tear and tear away at it ferociously, relentlessly, knowing that after this final spurt of vitality all my strength will be gone. The muscles in my arms and in my jaw start to jam. I am shaking to the core and weakening.

But then, contrary to all expectation, just as I have started to give up all hope, a little rent starts to appear in the orange-coloured fabric. Another tear is added to the first. I start to devour the fibres of the fabric with the appetite of a wolf. I stick my trembling fingers between the threads and start to tear away at the cloth.

I hear a final cracking sound, and then start to fall freely through the air. With a quick stroke of the tongue, the Seine swallows me up into its freezing entrails. The shock of the cold withdraws what little breath I have left. Gorged with water, the knot tightens around my throat once again. I manage to loosen it enough to let a few mouthfuls of water enter my windpipe.

My lungs full of Seine, I sink, flailing, lashing out in every direction in the invasive depths of the water.

Gathering my strength, I tear at the liquid body with my nails. Rejecting death, I cast it aside. I palm it, stir it, again and again. I kick, scratch at it, lunging with my head. I strike out and slap. I push it down with all my strength. And then, suddenly, against all expectation, despite the fact that the light still seems much too far away, I burst out at the surface.

But the current pushes my head back under as soon as I emerge under the speed of its flow. I no longer have the stamina to fight it off. The water pulls me by its irresistible scarf. I hit the arm of the water, I strike at it over and over, more and more feebly, my strength running out. The mouth of the water screams and something strikes back at me.

The arm around my neck lets go at last and I throw up the Seine in my lungs onto the bank. Two arms crush my chest. At the other end of the arms, a one-eyed, hairy face, dripping with anxiety. A single cyclopean eye. Tiresias.

"You came close to drowning me with you, you little runt", he says, still panting on the embankment, wringing the water out of his beard like a salt and pepper sponge. "Anyway, never mind. You're breathing, that's the main thing. You must be out of your mind, attempting an ordeal by water without me ... You could have got yourself killed!"

"That's what I was trying to do."

"It's a good job Cocteau called me as soon as you left his hotel room. He was right to be alarmed ... You're lucky I guessed you'd come here. Anyway, that was pretty insane."

"I really thought I was going to end up not drowned but hanged under water."

"Yeah, I saw you dangling and struggling at the end of that orange sheet of yours. I was running up to deliver you when it tore and you fell like a bombshell. I had to run like mad on the bank before jumping into the water. And to top that, you almost drowned me with your punches!"

"Forgive me. I'm so sorry ..."

"You should cover yourself up, you're stark naked. What's this watered orange fabric?"

"It's a gown I stole in Siam."

"Wait, I'm going to help you untie the knot. We can make a loincloth out of this. You'll look like one of Gauguin's Christ figures."

"I'm so sorry about all this. I suddenly felt such a strong urge to live. It's barely believable, for someone like me. All that hidden yearning, stuffed under the surface. I would never have thought it. I had a kind of revelation this time. I was both submerged by fear and calm at the same time. And all of a sudden I felt, as if by magic, that all my world-weariness was dissolving in the water. The first jump you made me attempt took away a good part of my inhibitions. I think the second jump has cleansed me of Jean, of all my excesses. My crisis."

"I experienced some of the same things as you when I was your age, a little older perhaps. I found myself estranged. Without a girlfriend, without parents. Well, they lived far away, in Bucharest. I had come to seek my fortune in Paris la Belle. In Romania, people see France as a kind of Eldorado. In those days, I was scared of sinking into oblivion. It was my greatest fear. Romania was unexciting to me. I found it provincial, devoid of taste. I used to read Jules Verne, Victor Hugo, Alexandre Dumas, and from time to time, a more recent author, chosen among the very few who made it to our bookstores. And I chafed at the bit. Like you, I wanted to become a writer. I was also very shy. I used to tell myself that literature was the mouthpiece of those that nature had burdened with inhibition. A compensation for those who couldn't speak up in society. I wanted a life that wouldn't be mundane and in a sense I got that, but not thanks to writing. I quickly—perhaps too quickly—faced the obvious truth: that I was little more than a pen-pusher. You need such a huge quantity of work and courage, such massive quantities of perseverance to become a writer ... especially when it isn't your own language. Bloody hell! I can't seem to open this knot. I'm going to have to cut it open. Let's see ... Don't be scared, I'm not going to slit your throat after saving your life. Anyway, I doubted my talents so much at the time that I lost the will to pursue my goals. When I realized I wouldn't be able to become a writer as easily as I thought I would, I surrounded myself with artists instead. But before finding that path, I can tell you I suffered the same torments you've endured. I went through some really rough times ... There, just a few more threads and we're done."

"I'll tear the rest."

"You're right, you go ahead and do that ... I leave you the honour of severing the cord. Ah, at last. There we are. Now, make yourself a loincloth out of that part. You must be freezing."

"Not really, especially not after having fought against the water. I was in such a panic I couldn't feel the cold. I'm actually a bit hot ..."

"Go on, admit it, I see you're asking yourself if it was in that period of my life that I lost my eye ... You don't need to be embarrassed. You know, I've told nobody. Mostly because nobody dares to mention it. I did lose it back then. I was experiencing a lot of anguish. I was in exile, far from everything. I had a pretty strong accent in French. I would make the most grotesque errors, which put off a lot of employers. I had to go

from one drudging, poorly-paid, dead-end job
to another. I must have sent my two first novels
to more than forty publishers. Everything was
going to the dogs. And little by little I started
wanting to end it all, without really realizing.
One day, the idea of suicide entered my head,
a new idea that had never occurred to me. At
least, never seriously. Before that, people who
committed suicide seemed to belong to another
world, a place peopled by lunatics, sickos,
unfathomable individuals. And suddenly, I
could understand them. I was one of them. And
I didn't feel sick or particularly demented, but I
knew I now belonged to that category of people,
the oversensitive, the weak, despite my body
mass. Anyway, I was scrawnier back then, so
was my beard. Every time I crossed a bridge, I
was afraid an uncontrollable urge would throw
me into the Seine. In fact, on several occasions,
I very nearly pitched myself off the same bridge
you chose ..."

"Is that why you got me to jump off, that
first time?"

"I don't know. It's possible ... It was mostly
so that you would understand what I fathomed
too late at my own expense. Because this is
where I lost my eye."

"On this very spot?"

"Yes, well, over there, on Mirabeau Bridge.
That day, I was in one of my self-destructive
states. I had gazed at myself in a mirror coming

home from work one evening and I just couldn't stand the sight of my face. It seemed unbearably bland to me, even with the beard. So, I resolved to blind myself, so I wouldn't have to contemplate my ugly mug in the mirror. I took out my knife. Yes, this one ... I stuck the tip of it between my eyelid and the eyeball and I cut out the jelly. I made the whole thing come out of the socket. It actually came out pretty easily. I had decided to take the other one out too, but thankfully I grew fearful. And the pain was excruciating. There was blood all over the place. A real nightmare. I went out into the streets in the dead of the night, stained like a pig, with my eye in my hand, looking for goodness knows what. In any case, I didn't find it. When I got to Mirabeau Bridge, I got up on the handrail to throw myself into the Seine. But in the end, instead of jumping I threw my eye into the bottom of the river. I still had that yearning to end it all; but some unknown inner force held me back. The same survival instinct, I suppose, that stopped me from taking out my second eye. And then it occurred to me that there was already a part of my body at the bottom of the water. A sufficient sacrifice unto itself."

We remain silent, gazing at the shimmering reflections of the dawn flitting over the water.

"That's it ... Of course I regret it a little, especially when I feel the painful throbbing at the root of my optical nerve, but that horri-

fying moment sharpened my sight, so to speak.
After that incident, I started seeing things with
different eyes, both literally and figuratively. So
there you are, you know the story now. You're
one of the few who do, along with Cocteau.
Actually, I never gave him a full account, but I
think he has a good inkling."

"He told me your real name isn't Tiresias."

"Oh, really? It's true. I took on that name
after the loss of my eye. To compensate for it
in some way. It was a literary name, a byword
for clairvoyance. I hesitated between Tiresias
and Odin. I opted for the first one in the end,
I can't remember why exactly. I said to myself
that with a single eye, I would have to be
clairvoyant."

"What was your name before that?"

"My Christian name? Eugene. I used to find
it so common. These days, I rather like it, but
everyone knows me as Tiresias and it would feel
strange to go back to where I started. Anyway,
I have the impression that we learnt the same
thing, something you can't really explain. You
feel it inside you, like an underground stream."

"I know what you mean. I still have some of
it in my lungs."

I cough a little and we laugh as if a burden
has been lifted.

"So, it looks like you won't be needing a
mentor now. Do come and see me some time,
all the same. I'll be eager to get some news from

time to time. You'll know where to find me, in any case, even if it's in a few years."

"Still so expeditious, my good old Tiresias. I missed you. I promise to come and see you, alone or in company."

"Ha! Right after drowning, he's already thinking of seduction. That's really great. You have to know how to keep up the charm right 'til the end. Don't forget to put some clothes on, though. You wouldn't want people to take you for Jesus. Might end badly. See you, Thomas. Good luck."

Mr. Tiresias is already moving off, like a passer-by who has lent a helping hand to push a broken-down automobile. The moment it starts and the passer-by is thanked for his efforts, he pursues his original path with a brief wave of the hand as a sign of farewell. He didn't even ask me any questions about Indochina, as if he already knew all there was to know.

And I, the holy terror, take up the torch again, having been stopped before I could commit irreparable foolishness. Now that I no longer wish to hang myself, I don't know where I will go. But it no longer matters. I do not know what the future holds in store, but after all the ordeals I've had to endure I feel ready for anything. Come what may. And I finally know what I want.

Putting on my clothes again, I come upon the two letters in my coat. I had forgotten them since my transformation as a monk. The first, from Cocteau, is already unsealed, consumed, spent, a dead letter now; the other, from the young woman met on the quay of Bangkok, sealed, still full of promise, bent in the pocket of my coat like a bow aimed at the future. I'm tempted, once again, to open it to discover the contents, but the girl's smile has entrusted this.

I open my one again, one last time. I read it for the hundredth time, without pain, without resentment, smiling like the young woman on the quay. Just a smile delicately placing its lips on the past. I look at it like the parent of the child I used to be hardly an hour ago.

"Don't be timid ... if the evening is impossible."

I rip it slowly, ceremoniously, with respect for the old me, the old Jean Cocteau. The pieces quiver slightly in the palm of my hand. The morning breeze tries to waft them away. I'm going to shred it into tiny pieces over the Seine. They will flutter away like confetti for a marriage that will never happen.

Despite the longing, despite myself, I am unable to throw the pieces overboard. They remain there, sealed in my fist.

I let them slip one by one from my hand to the bottom of the bag.

Taking out my wallet, I place one of my stamps on the young woman's envelope. It slips unimpeded into the slit of the letterbox.

Erik Martiny (born 11 June 1971) is a Franco-Irish-Swedish novelist, academic and journalist who teaches at the Lycée Henri IV in Paris. His reviews on art and literature have appeared in *The Cambridge Quarterly, The Times Literary Supplement, Whitewall Magazine, The London Magazine,* and *Aesthetica Magazine.* He is the author of seven previous works of fiction, including *Night of the Long Goodbyes* (2020), *Crown of Beaks* (2021), *Waiting for Gaudiya and Other Stories* (2021), and *The Moose, the Mouse, and the Little Irish Boy* (2021), which he co-authored with his son.